What the critics are saying...

"Ms. Burton has an amazing ability to build the heat in the story between her characters and when things finally happen, WOW! *Magnolia Summer* will be a great addition to your bedside and this contemporary erotic romance will have you chuckling away and hotter than hot!" ~ *Julie Esparza Just Erotic Romance Reviews*

5 Angels "*Magnolia Summer* is a poignant story that will pull on your heartstrings and stay with you after the last page is read...Jaci Burton creates an unforgettable tale that will have you thinking about fate and destiny and how it can, or already has influenced your own life. If you are looking for an unforgettable and emotional love story, this reviewer highly recommends Magnolia Summer by Jaci Burton." ~ *Cindy Fallen Angels Reviews*

"...Hot summer nights have never been as hot as in the pages of *Magnolia Summer*. Drown in the outstanding passion, heart and emotion as only Jaci Burton writes it. As always she leaves her reader begging for more of the same. *Magnolia Summer*...it sends temperatures soaring!" ~ *Tracey West for Road to Romance*

5 RIBBON REVIEW "MAGNOLIA SUMMER is an awesome book and you won't be able to put it down until you finish it. Readers who come from small towns will love this in-depth look at small town life...with MAGNOLIA SUMMER...Jaci Burton has once again written a story with interesting characters and a magnetic plot that will pull you in." ~ *Angel Brewer Romance Junkies.*

MAGNOLIA SUMMER

By Jaci Burton

MAGNOLIA SUMMER
An Ellora's Cave Publication, April 2005

Ellora's Cave Publishing, Inc.
1337 Commerce Drive
Stow, Ohio 44224

ISBN #1419951580
Other available formats: ISBN MS Reader (LIT), Adobe (PDF),
Rocketbook (RB), Mobipocket (PRC) & HTML

Edited by: *Briana St. James*
Cover art by: *Syneca*

Warning:

The following material contains graphic sexual content meant for mature readers. *Magnolia Summer* has been rated *E-rotic* by a minimum of three independent reviewers.

Ellora's Cave Publishing offers three levels of Romantica™ reading entertainment: S (S-ensuous), E (E-rotic), and X (X-treme).

S-*ensuous* love scenes are explicit and leave nothing to the imagination.

E-*rotic* love scenes are explicit, leave nothing to the imagination, and are high in volume per the overall word count. In addition, some E-rated titles might contain fantasy material that some readers find objectionable, such as bondage, submission, same sex encounters, forced seductions, etc. E-rated titles are the most graphic titles we carry; it is common, for instance, for an author to use words such as "fucking", "cock", "pussy", etc., within their work of literature.

X-*treme* titles differ from E-rated titles only in plot premise and storyline execution. Unlike E-rated titles, stories designated with the letter X tend to contain controversial subject matter not for the faint of heart.

MAGNOLIA SUMMER

By Jaci Burton

Dedication

To Charlie. This one's all yours. If not for you, I'd never have started this book, which to this day remains a special one for both of us. If not for you, I'd never have found the magical love that inspires me. You're the reason for this book, and you're the reason for my happiness. I love you, babe.

Chapter One

Jordan Weston drew a deep breath as she stood outside, staring intently at the sign that said *TNT Construction*.

It was bad enough she had to be here in Magnolia. The town held nothing but bitter memories for her and the sooner she got out, the better. She had a life waiting for her back in New York. South Carolina may have been where she was born and raised, but it wasn't her home anymore.

One more task…one more huge task, and she'd be out of here. And if it meant walking through those doors and facing her past, she'd do it. Anything to get away from the memories.

She kicked her flagging courage in gear and walked through the doors, reminding herself her dream was at stake. It didn't matter who owned *TNT Construction*, she needed the company to do the job. And if it required her to see Sam again, so be it.

The air conditioning was a welcome relief from the humid South Carolina summer heat. A young, attractive blonde sat behind a large oak desk in the center of the office and smiled at her.

"Can I help you?" the woman asked, the lashes on her blue eyes loaded with so much mascara it was a wonder she could even see.

Fashion in small-town South Carolina was quite different than New York City. Had Jordan ever dressed the same way as the woman sitting at the desk? Had she worn too much makeup? It had been so long she couldn't remember.

Or, like most things about Magnolia, she didn't want to remember.

"Yes, I'm here to see Sam Tanner." The last person Jordan wanted to see in Magnolia, but she had no choice. He was the only one who could help her.

"Do you have an appointment?"

"No, I'm sorry I don't. I'm inquiring about hiring the company for a project."

The woman picked up the phone, her long painted fingernails tapping one of the buttons. "I'll let Sam know you're here. Can I have your name?"

"Jordan Weston." He probably didn't even remember her. Fourteen years was a long time. And they hadn't even dated. She'd simply been another one of the girls Sam had annoyed and teased.

Except for that one time.

Once he had kissed her.

It probably hadn't meant anything to Sam. But it had meant everything to Jordan's sixteen-year-old heart. Wrapped up in that kiss was desire, yearning, and those first feelings of love. Everything a girl dreamed about.

But that first crush, her first kiss, was a long time ago.

A lot had happened since then. She'd changed, and the simple crises of life in Magnolia weren't as critical any longer.

What *was* critical was getting the house fixed up and sold so she could get the hell out of here again.

The receptionist hung up and looked at Jordan. "Someone will be with you shortly. Please take a seat."

Taking a seat near the window, Jordan turned to look outside. Magnolia hadn't changed much since she'd been gone, its small-town ambience and charm still evident in the quaint brick and frame buildings lining Main Street, their signs proudly proclaiming family-owned businesses.

She remembered the trips into town on Saturdays and shopping with Grandma when she was little. They came almost every weekend, and the shop merchants knew her well, sometimes giving her candy. Those were the good memories.

Every memory of time spent with her grandmother was a good one. Now that Grandma was gone, she could forever cut her ties to this place.

After Grandma's funeral last month, she never planned to return to Magnolia. Grandma was her last surviving link to the town, and her one and only real parent. Jordan's mother had always been too wrapped up in screwing up her own life to take the time to raise her.

Grandma always told Jordan to live her life, and never look back. And she had. That's why she went to New York in the first place and why she didn't return except for occasional visits to see Grandma.

Over the years, her trips had slowed, and finally stopped. Grandma loved New York and Jordan brought her up to visit a couple times a year, making sure to score tickets to the latest musicals.

Until Grandma had gotten too old and too frail to make the journey, and Jordan hadn't been able to bring herself to return to Magnolia. Grandma had understood, but Jordan would never forgive herself for not seeing Grandma one last time.

Now here she was, back again. The news from Grandma's attorney forced her to return, at least for awhile. Which was why she was at TNT Construction and preparing to see Sam Tanner again.

The double doors behind the reception area opened. Jordan heard two men's voices just inside, but couldn't see either of them. She took a deep breath and waited.

He wasn't going to remember her, she was certain. And it was only one kiss. Hardly memorable at all. To him.

A deep voice bellowed from behind the door. "That's bullshit, Tony, and you know it. The project was bid and accepted over six months ago. Tell the clients to get up off their dead asses, quit trying to screw us over on the price and let's get moving on it."

"That's what I'm *trying* to do, you moron. You don't have to scream in my ear." A tall, good-looking man with sandy blond hair and bedroom brown eyes strolled through the doorway. "I'm not deaf, you know." He turned and paused to smile at the receptionist, clearly not upset at all by the altercation that just occurred. "Later, Cookie."

"Later, Tony," the receptionist replied in a breathy voice, her lustful gaze following the attractive man towards the door.

Cookie? The girl's name was Cookie? Jordan fought back a laugh.

Tony paused at the door and noticed Jordan sitting there. "Somebody helping you, honey?"

Jordan stood to address him but before she could respond, a voice from the doorway announced, "I'll take care of her." She couldn't see who was speaking because Tony blocked her view.

Tony looked over his shoulder and then back at Jordan, grinning broadly. "Yeah, I'm sure you will. What a shame, honey. You'd have liked me better." He winked at her and left.

As soon as Tony left, Jordan saw the other man. She wished she was still sitting because the vision greeting her almost knocked her off her feet.

Six-foot-two of drop-dead gorgeous man filled the doorway. He wore a TNT Construction polo shirt stretched tight across his chest and jeans that fit his muscled thighs like a second skin. His hair was jet black, cut short and straight. Turquoise eyes glittered with light, just like the ocean she'd seen on a trip to Mexico. This guy could be a New York model in a heartbeat. Beefcake like that didn't go unnoticed in the fashion world there.

He was nothing like Jordan remembered. If anything, he was more handsome now than he'd ever been in high school.

She'd expected him to age badly. Or maybe she had just hoped he would. Instead, he'd grown into his body and had gone from good-looking boy to damned breathtaking man.

It figured.

"Well," he said, leisurely strolling over to stand in front of Jordan, towering over her five foot six inches. "Jordan Lee Weston, big city girl, back in Magnolia." His lethal smile and penetrating eyes still took her breath away.

"Sam," she replied in a voice that sounded too low and sexy to be her own. Breathe, Jordan, breathe. You can face the sharks in New York City, you sure as hell can handle small-town lover boy Sam Tanner.

"It's been a long time." His deep, resonating voice settled over her, warming her from the inside out. Melting the icy wall she had built, sparking a long dormant flame to life.

"Yes, it has." So he's still hot—no, hotter—than you remembered. Think business. Think money. Think anything but his piercing eyes, and the way he smells, so masculine, so overwhelmingly…potent.

What was wrong with her? She should say something, but her mind was a blank. She was, after all, a *magna cum laude* graduate who was usually never at a loss for words. Until now, standing to face with the man of her girlhood fantasies. A man who had matured beyond the boyish good looks of high school, into a very tall, devastating specimen of masculinity.

"Let's go to my office," he said, breaking the spell that had rendered her temporarily mute.

Jordan followed Sam through the doorway, noticing Cookie's eyebrows arch in curiosity as she passed by. Ah yes, the gossip mill's wheels were beginning to turn already. She could only imagine what was going through the young woman's mind at the moment, but wagered Cookie would be picking up the phone shortly in an attempt to gather information about Jordan.

Sam directed her into his spacious office behind the reception area. A large oak desk sat in the middle of the room, two gray cloth chairs placed in front. The credenza was neatly stacked with papers on the left and a computer in the center. Organized, wasn't he?

A large picture window provided an ample view of Main Street's activity. Sam motioned for her to take a seat as he sat behind the desk.

"Let's see," he said in a voice much deeper than Jordan remembered. "Last time I saw you was at the Spring Fling Dance. You were a junior and I was a senior. I cornered you in the hall outside the gym, gave you one seriously hot kiss, and you ran like a scared rabbit."

He did remember. Damn.

"You still have that frightened rabbit look about you, Jordan. Surely you're not afraid of me now, are you?" His killer smile made Jordan feel much warmer than she should in the cool office.

Jordan lifted her chin. "I was never afraid of you," she lied. Not much anyway. Sam terrified her back then. Made her want things she had no business wanting.

Things she hadn't thought about since she'd left town after graduation. Things she didn't want to be thinking about now.

"I always wondered why you ran when I kissed you. It couldn't have been the kiss. None of the other girls ever ran away." He obviously thought himself quite amusing because he grinned. "In fact, I'd been told by those same girls that I was one hell of a kisser."

She wanted to laugh at his arrogance, but he wasn't lying. The other girls were right. Sam *was* one hell of a kisser. Enough to fire up Jordan's teenage sex drive and flame a desire she'd never felt before. Enough to make her run.

Jordan shrugged off his comments. "It's been fourteen years, Sam. I hardly remember that kiss." Yeah, right. Only every time someone else kissed her. And not one ever came close to generating the fire stirred by that kiss all those years ago.

She still remembered his lips sliding over hers, claiming her, possessing her, his tongue exploring the recesses of her mouth and igniting her youthful passions until she realized what she'd been doing and ran like hell.

"Well, maybe you don't, but I remember it well." His eyes held hers for a moment, and Jordan thought she saw some flicker of emotion pass through them, but then it disappeared. "You here on business, Jordan, or just want to catch up on old times?" The sensuous look in his eyes was gone. He smiled at her in an easy manner.

How quickly he could turn the charm on and off. Typical for men like him. "I came to talk to you about Belle Coeur. I've inherited the estate and it needs some repair."

"I heard about Viola's passing, Jordan. I was out of town and couldn't make the funeral. I'm very sorry."

"Thank you," she said, noticing the expression of sympathy on his face. She looked away, not wanting to feel the pain of grieving over Grandma. "Anyway, I'd like to hire TNT Construction to do the repairs."

That was really a lie, too. Jordan didn't want to have anything to do with Sam Tanner, but she'd already found out TNT was the only company in town capable of the extensive work needed on Belle Coeur.

"What kind of repairs are we talking about?" Sam took out a yellow notepad and grabbed a pen from the cup on his desk.

She crossed her legs and sat back in the chair, relaxing a bit now that the subject was on the house and not their kiss. "I really have no idea. I know the place is in disrepair, and probably requires a lot of work, but I don't know exactly what needs to be done."

Sam's gaze followed her movements, shifting to her legs before he quickly looked up, a smile curving his generous lips. She pulled at the hem of her short cotton skirt, wishing she had worn pants instead.

"It depends on what your plans are for the property."

"I intend to sell Belle Coeur."

"Sell it?" Surprise clearly showed on his face. "Are you sure that's what Viola would have wanted? I thought Belle Coeur had been in your family for generations."

She nodded, ignoring the stab of guilt. "Yes, it has, but I have no intention of coming back here to live. My life is somewhere else now, and that's where I intend to stay. I have plans."

Big plans. With the money she'd make from the sale of Belle Coeur, she could realize her dream of starting a theater in New York. She pushed aside the pangs of regret she felt whenever she thought about selling her family home, refusing to give into emotion. This was a business decision.

"Ah yes, New York, isn't it?" At her affirmative nod, he continued. "Home of the theater. Right up your dramatic alley isn't it?" His tone was sarcastic, and Jordan could just imagine what he was thinking. Geeky high school Drama Club president seeks fame and fortune in New York.

She smiled, betraying nothing of her irritation at his comments. "Why yes, as a matter of fact it is."

"Thought you'd get over that whole theater thing after high school. Guess not."

Her ire rising by the moment, she shot back, "Thought you'd get over being a sarcastic asshole after high school. Guess not."

A wry smile curved those generous lips. "Touché. So you're still in theater, I take it?"

"Yes, Assistant Director at the Manhattan Community Playhouse." At least for now. Until she could buy her own company. Then she'd be an owner, able to produce and direct her own plays.

"What? You're not an actress?"

Somehow the way he said *actress* sounded like an insult. Now she was getting annoyed. "Do you have some problem with my choice of career?"

His grin widened, irritating the hell out of her. "Would it matter to you if I did?"

Despite wanting to slap the grin off his face, she shook her head and graced him with a benign smile. "Not in the least. Would it matter to you if I thought you were an arrogant prick?"

Mimicking her response, he said lightly, "Not in the least."

Now she remembered how much he'd aggravated her in high school, always teasing and embarrassing her. The one boy she had a fierce crush on, and he thought of her as a drama nerd. Apparently still did. Just like Magnolia, Sam hadn't changed.

"I'd like to keep this relationship professional, Sam. We don't have a history together, in fact weren't even friends. Now are you interested in my business, or should I take it elsewhere?"

Sam rose and approached her. She stood, the instinct to back away warring with the desire to stand her ground and show Sam she wasn't afraid of being close to him. Even if her heart was pounding.

Enigmatic turquoise eyes captured her. She wanted to look away, but couldn't.

"Sorry, you can't take your business elsewhere. I'm the only game in town, so it looks like you're stuck with me. Now if you'd like, I'll come by tomorrow, take a look at the place and give you a bid on repairs."

He'd come by? Didn't he have other people to do those kinds of things for him? The thought of having to see him yet again unnerved her.

"Couldn't you send someone else?"

The corners of his mouth lifted. "Why? Are you afraid to be alone with me?"

Damn. Why did she ask him that? Jordan refused to be afraid of him. Let him come by and do the estimate himself. After all, she had no lingering feelings for him. Maybe if she kept telling herself that she'd begin to believe it. Fat chance.

"Of course I'm not afraid to be alone with you. I just don't like your attitude."

Sam laughed at her. "My attitude? You mean my interest, don't you?"

"Interest? Hardly." Sam was no more interested in her than she was in him.

"I think I still scare you Jordan, but is it because you're afraid of men, afraid of me, or afraid of yourself?"

Their gazes locked and she wondered if he had any idea how close he'd come to pinpointing all of her fears.

When she didn't answer he shrugged. "But if you don't trust yourself to be alone with me, I'll be happy to send Tony."

Jordan sensed she'd been set up. If she asked him to send Tony, Sam would know it had something to do with how she felt about him. And she'd be damned if she'd turn tail and run now. This wasn't high school, and she wasn't afraid of him. She tried to appear nonchalant. "Send whoever you want. It doesn't matter one way or the other to me."

"Then I'll see you tomorrow morning. I'll be by early."

"Fine. See you then." She caught the flicker of amusement on his face, wanted to stop and say something, but decided against it. Pausing at the double doors leading to the reception area, she drew in a deep breath and blew it out in the hopes of calming her ragged nerves.

Why, after all these years, did he still have an effect on her?

* * * * *

Sam turned on the lamp and sat behind his desk. He glanced at his watch and saw it was already nine o'clock. Another late night. No wonder he hadn't been laid in ages. How was he supposed to date a girl, let alone get one in the sack, when work consumed his entire life? He made a mental note to do something about that as soon as he could.

Then maybe his mind wouldn't wander over the past, over a woman who could never be his. He shook his head. Just like high school. He couldn't have her then, and he couldn't now, either.

Jordan Weston. No wonder he was thinking about getting fucked. Seeing her again after all these years did a number on his libido. And that he hadn't expected. He no longer had teenage hormones to contend with, but he sure as hell felt the slam in his gut when he saw her today. It was like all those years had been wiped away, and they were back at the dance again. He could still remember the taste of her lips. So sweet, so innocent, yet with a sultry promise of something more.

Something he'd wanted so badly he could still remember how it felt. But that was all in the past, and that's where it had to stay.

She had grown up to become a beautiful woman. But he always knew she would. In high school, her beauty had just begun to blossom.

Back then his friends would have laughed at him if they had known how he felt. He could imagine their reaction if they ever found out the high school bad boy had a crush on the Drama Club president.

So no one had ever known. Not even Jordan. Especially not Jordan. She was so smart and pretty. Fresh and innocent, the first blush of the beauty she'd become just beginning to appear. Sam did what he had to in order to save himself. Teased her, unmercifully. Annoyed her, irritated her, did anything he could to push her away.

Every time she'd graced him with those sparkling emerald eyes, a mixture of young love and desire reflected in their depths, it shook him to the core. It was obvious Jordan cared for him. And that he couldn't allow. He wasn't right for her.

A knock on the door switched Sam's mind back to the present. Tony strolled in and plopped down on a chair, stretching his lanky legs out.

"So?" Tony looked at him expectantly.

"So what?"

"Tell me about the gorgeous redhead who was in here this morning. Man, was she hot."

Sam shook his head as he regarded the grin on his best friend's face. Tony thought he was irresistible to most of the female population of the world. He was usually right. His charm and obvious appreciation for members of the opposite sex kept his social calendar full.

"Nothing to tell. She wants some repairs done to Viola Lake's property so she came in to ask for an estimate."

"And?"

"And what?"

"You know her. That much is obvious."

"We went to high school together. That's all."

"Really. Seemed to me there was more than that." One eyebrow arched in interest. Tony was clearly looking for sordid details.

He grabbed a few papers from his desk and began signing documents, trying to avoid eye contact. Tony always knew when he was lying. "No, there really wasn't anything else. She was a drama student in school. We had nothing in common except that we shared some classes. She wasn't my type. Still isn't."

"Right. Stunningly beautiful redheads with long legs and perfect breasts aren't your type."

Damn. Caught him again.

Sam smiled. "You're right. I lied. She is beautiful. But she's still not my type. She lives in New York."

"Oh, I see. City girl, huh?"

"Yeah."

Rising and stretching his back, Tony headed toward the door. "You're right then. Definitely not your type. Maybe I'll ask her out." Sam watched the gleam form in his friend's eyes, a look he had seen all too often when Tony set his mind on a new conquest.

The thought of Tony hitting on Jordan, touching her, or God forbid kissing her, sent a large green-eyed monster racing through his blood.

"Save it," Sam said bluntly. "You'll never make it past her front door."

Tony regarded him for a few minutes, his expression unfathomable. "Ohhkay. It's a shame though. What a beauty. Well, see you tomorrow."

Sam said goodnight to Tony and went back to his paperwork. Only now he was thoroughly distracted. Visions of the woman who wasn't his type kept appearing before him.

She'd matured into the beauty he'd had known she'd become. Jordan had a face men wrote poetry about—creamy complexion, full, kissable lips, and a pert nose with a light sprinkling of freckles across the bridge. And her eyes mesmerized him. The emerald orbs sparkled with a brightness and clarity unequaled by any gem of matching color. Framing that beautiful face was a shining array of long, auburn hair that a man's hands could get lost in.

And her body, well now that was a work of art.

The woman had curves in all the right places, a beautifully rounded ass and full, high breasts that just begged to be touched. And kissed, and licked.

But her best assets were her legs—long and slender with shapely calves. Sam could visualize those legs wrapping around his waist as he sank deep within her moist heat.

Dammit. Not only was he waxing like some goddamn poet over Jordan's beauty, he'd also sprouted a painful erection just thinking about her.

Christ.

This wasn't high school, and she wasn't his type at all. He had his fill of women who thought small towns were for hicks and hillbillies. Women who were attracted to the glamour and flash of a big city just weren't for him. He needed someone who would be satisfied with what he had to offer. Here, in Magnolia.

Jordan was already counting the minutes until she could get out of town. A woman like that would never be for him.

After neatly stacking the papers on his desk, he rose and turned off the lamp. But instead of walking out the door, he stood in the dark, staring out the window at the deserted Main Street. And thought about Jordan.

No matter how he felt about her in high school, things were different now. Despite having an incredible yearning to touch her, kiss her lush lips and taste the treasures within, Sam faced reality.

He was small town and she was big city. And he'd never do big city again. Not after what Penny did to him. Oh sure, Sam liked women. But only for fun and sex. Not for long-term involvement, not until he found one who'd be happy here in Magnolia. Sam wasn't going to get burned again.

So he'd give her a bid on repairs to Belle Coeur, and if she accepted he'd send a crew out to do the job, but that was it. There was no way in hell Sam would get involved with Jordan Weston.

Chapter Two

A distant ringing roused Jordan from a restful, dreamless slumber. Not fully coherent, she thought it was the phone next to her bed, but when she picked it up there was only a dial tone. She flipped onto her stomach and pulled the pillow over her head to drown out the sound.

The incessant jingle continued until Jordan could ignore it no longer. She whipped over and sat up abruptly, running her fingers through her hair and trying to focus herself into consciousness. The doorbell, that's what it was. What time was it, anyway? From the look of the sky outside the window next to her bed, it appeared to be somewhere between dark and darker.

She jumped out of bed and slowly made her way down the stairs as the annoying sound continued to clamor in her ears.

"I'm coming, I'm coming!" she shouted to whoever was leaning on the doorbell. "Give me a minute, dammit, I'm coming!"

She flung open the door and immediately wished she hadn't. Standing there looking freshly shaved, wide-awake and grinning stupidly, was Sam.

"You're not up yet?"

"Well I am now," she replied without humor, her eyes still making an attempt to focus. "What are you doing here so early? What time is it? It's not even dawn."

Sam leaned against the doorway, clearly unaffected by the fact it was the crack of dawn and he'd just roused her from her bed. "I'm here because you asked me to come, it's six-thirty and high time for most folks to be up and at it. Besides, I told you I'd come by early."

Jordan yawned. "Six-thirty is too early. Come back when it's daylight." She started to close the door in his face, but Sam blocked it with his hand.

"I don't think so." He gently pushed the door open and stepped into the foyer. "First off, I'm already here and that means I'm staying. Second, you just need some coffee and a good hot breakfast and you'll be wide awake." Gripping her shoulders, he turned her around and directed her toward the kitchen. "Go on and sit down. We can talk while I get coffee and breakfast going."

When she didn't immediately move, Sam shut the front door and headed into the kitchen, shouting behind him that he knew the way.

Jordan stared dumbfounded at Sam's retreating form. What just happened here? Was she still asleep and having a nightmare? She thought for a moment, and decided she was definitely awake. A waking nightmare, that was it.

She walked down the long hallway toward the oversized kitchen. As she entered, her nightmare was spooning coffee into a filter and pouring water in the coffeemaker. He stopped and looked up at her.

"You like it strong? Wakes you up faster, you know." He waited for a response, but she had nothing to say. Shrugging, he continued. "Well, I'll just make it the way I like it, and you can see if it's the way you like it." Giving her a sly smile, he said, "I bet we like things the same way. What do you think?"

This was unbelievable. Jordan stood in the doorway, hands on her hips. "What I think is that I asked you to leave. What I think is that you are rude and unprofessional to come barging into my house and making yourself at home as if you lived here. What I think is that my original invitation for you to come back later still stands. And if you don't mind, I think you should leave!"

He didn't even look up as he grabbed eggs and bacon from the refrigerator and set them on the counter near the stove. "No, I don't mind at all. I cook breakfast for myself all the time, although I didn't have time to do it this morning. I'm starving, aren't you?"

Jordan threw her hands up in the air. Sam was obviously so dense he couldn't even figure out she was yelling at him. Anger rendered her speechless. She glared at him for several minutes, hoping he'd get the hint and leave. It wasn't happening.

As the eggs and bacon sizzled, Sam turned and looked Jordan up and down, arching his brows in appreciation. "My, my, Jordan, you sure do make a hot picture first thing in the morning. Maybe I'll come over early and make breakfast for you every day."

The way he looked at her hit Jordan like a splash of cold water. She realized the old white cotton T-shirt she wore didn't leave much, if anything, to the imagination. Since she figured Sam had a pretty good imagination, she immediately sat down to retain what little modesty she had left.

"Would you please get out!" She pointed to the door.

Sam laughed. "I'm just teasing you, Jordan. Boy you're easy to get riled, especially before you've had a cup of coffee." As he said it, he placed a steaming cup before her. "You want milk or sugar?"

It was pointless to try and get him to listen. Perhaps he didn't understand simple English, like get out, get lost and go away. She finally gave up.

"I can get my own coffee." She started to stand up, but then remembering her state of minimal dress, quickly sat down again. Feeling trapped behind the table, she figured the only way to get rid of him was let him have his way. "Milk would be fine," she answered tightly. Sam smiled wickedly and set the milk on the table in front of her.

"Should have made you get it yourself," he said through his wide grin. "I would have enjoyed the view."

Jordan sighed, exasperated with him already, and he hadn't been there more than ten minutes. Was sex the only thing men like him thought about? How typical, and how right she was never to get involved with someone like him. Charming men like Sam were only interested in one thing, and once they got it they moved on to the next conquest. Look what a man like that had done to her mother. Jordan would never make the same mistake.

The smell of bacon made her stomach rumble. As she sipped her coffee she watched Sam cook. Damn, but he was spectacular looking. His back was turned to her, and she got a good look at his wide shoulders, strong back, and lean, muscled legs. He was wearing a pair of old faded Levis and a blue sleeveless T-shirt stretched tight across his back. And what a rear end. If that kind of man interested her, she'd be all over him in a heartbeat.

Good thing Jordan was so involved with the other areas of her life she didn't need romance or great sex. Then again, she wouldn't know what great sex was if it came up and bit her. Her own choice of course, but she couldn't help having an occasional regret.

Lost in thought, she jumped and eyed Sam warily when he leaned over to place her breakfast on the table. He sat down in the chair next to her and began to eat. Suddenly ravenous, she picked up her fork and took a bite. Surprisingly, it was very good.

"When did you learn to cook?" she asked between mouthfuls.

"Cooking's not that hard. I learned to take care of myself a long time ago. Really learned to cook after my divorce."

"I didn't know you had been married. When was your divorce?" For some reason the fact he'd married hurt. But why? It wasn't like they'd had a torrid romance in high school, or any romance at all. They weren't sweethearts, they hadn't dated, and it was only one kiss.

Keep reminding yourself of that, Jordan.

"About three years ago." He looked up and smiled. "We met in college." At Jordan's surprised look, he said, "Yes, I went to college. Graduated too."

So many things about Sam she didn't know. Like where he had disappeared his senior year. After the dance she'd never seen him again.

"She was a small-town girl, and I thought our paths were headed in the same direction. I was wrong. We married when we were seniors and I brought her here when I started TNT. It wasn't a year before she was dreaming of bigger and better things."

"What kind of things?" Okay, maybe Jordan hadn't wanted to stay in Magnolia, either, but that didn't mean any other small-town girl couldn't be happy here.

"She wanted what I couldn't give her. What I really didn't want to give her. A big city, fancy shopping malls, prestige and lots of money. And I guess she decided that a life with me wasn't going to provide what she thought she needed. So she left. No big deal."

Sam had answered her question matter-of-factly, as if he didn't care at all about the woman who had once been his wife. "So, you just let her go, just like that?"

His gaze met hers, his expression devoid of emotion. "I wasn't going to try to hold onto someone who'd be happier somewhere else. We didn't really love each other anyway, so why prolong the inevitable? I was happy living here in Magnolia, and she wasn't. She had big city dreams and I wasn't going to move. End of story."

Jordan pushed her plate away and sat back, contemplating what Sam said. Why was he so happy here? He'd seemed so restless in high school. Granted, she wasn't his best friend back then but they'd shared some classes, and he'd always asked her to help him with homework.

His requests for tutoring had always surprised her because he was very intelligent. In classes he always knew the answers when asked. During times she helped him out they talked about what they wanted to do after graduation. He had told her he had big plans. Traveling, seeing exotic places, doing things he could never do here. His plan had been to leave Magnolia and never come back. True enough, he'd left. But he'd come back. Jordan wondered what changed his mind.

"Didn't you want to get out of this place after high school? I thought you wanted to travel."

Sam nodded and took a sip of coffee. "Yeah I did. And I saw the world, like I wanted to. Traveled around a lot, then came back home."

"Why did you come back?" She'd always thought he was just like her. Get out of Magnolia and never look back. She hadn't looked back. Not only had he looked back, he'd come back.

Gathering their dishes and cups, he put them into the sink and approached her, stopping inches away. She was almost afraid to breathe, knowing he'd smell freshly showered and more edible than the breakfast he'd just fixed.

He placed his arms on either side of her chair, forcing her to look up at him. His gaze was sharp and assessing, as if he knew her, could read her thoughts and emotions. Ridiculous, considering they were virtually strangers.

"Sometimes what you think you want out of life isn't what you really want at all. Get dressed, Jordan." He started down the hall to the front door. "I'm going to check out the front of the house. Meet me out there when you're ready and we'll figure out what needs to be done around here."

Some deep thoughts in his statement. Thoughts she didn't want to ponder, at least relating to her own reasons for doing things.

After he closed the front door, Jordan got up from the table and headed upstairs to change. Where had he gone when he left Magnolia all those years ago, and what had he been doing? What would bring someone back who had craved travel and adventure, who had counted the months until he could skip out of town?

He'd skipped out of town all right. And right off the face of the Earth. If his parents knew where he went, they didn't say, and no one could ever figure it out. Where did he go, and why did he come back?

And why the hell did she care? Clearly she'd get no answers today.

Pausing as she reached her bedroom, Jordan once again questioned her curiosity. Why did she care what Sam had been doing? She wasn't interested in him romantically; Sam was just someone she once knew in high school who was going to do a job for her. She didn't care what he had been doing, or why his marriage broke up.

Besides, he was everything she'd tried to avoid her entire life. A man like her father. Good-looking, charming. A heartbreaker. No one was going to break her heart. She'd guarded it for almost thirty years now, and not a single man had gotten close. The only one who had ever inched his way into her heart was now outside waiting for her to join him.

Stop wondering. Stop asking questions. Stop caring. She needed to concentrate on using Sam's expertise and skills to get Grandma's house—no, *her* house—repaired.

As soon as that was done, she could get out of Magnolia.

* * * * *

Sam retrieved his clipboard from the truck and turned around to look at the old house. Leaning back against the truck door, he waited for Jordan. He thought about how she looked when she answered the door this morning, her hair a tangled mess and wearing only a thin cotton T-shirt that barely covered her slender thighs. Her face had that sleepy, just-got-out-of-bed look he found so sexy.

When she'd opened the door, his heart leapt in his throat. He'd felt a sudden desire to pick up her sleepy form, climb the stairs to her bedroom and feel her warm body wrapped around him. He wondered what it would be like to wake up next to her after making love to her all night long.

With a disgusted curse, he adjusted his now tight jeans. He was never going to survive working around the woman if he couldn't keep from getting hard every time she was near. She wasn't even his type; she was just like Penny, with her dislike of small towns. And they were as mismatched as two people could be. Jordan was glamour, sophistication and parties; he was jeans, T-shirts and corner bars. He'd been down that road before, and wasn't going there again.

Just because she looked sexy, smelled good, and had a body he was dying to get his hands on was no reason to get all worked up. There were plenty of women more than willing to hook up with him, he just hadn't had time.

Well, he'd just have to start finding the time, and soon. Once he got laid five or six times he wouldn't think about Jordan at all.

The subject of Sam's thoughts opened the front door at that moment. She'd pulled her hair back in a ponytail, the long red strands swaying back and forth as she walked down the stairs. She wore blue jean shorts, sandals and an *I LOVE NY* T-shirt that barely covered her tanned, flat stomach.

Sam swallowed past the desert in his throat when he spotted the jeweled belly ring piercing her navel.

Goddamn, that was sexy as hell. Covering his aching hard-on with the clipboard, he tried to push aside thoughts of licking that pierced navel on his way further south.

She smiled, and it nearly devastated him. Although she'd been living the high life in New York, her face still bore the fresh, dewy complexion of a small-town girl.

The absence of makeup didn't detract from her appearance. Instead, it made her look youthful and fresh. And incredibly desirable.

His balls began to throb.

Go away, dick. You're not getting any right now, and sure as hell not from Jordan Weston.

This was going to be a helluva lot more difficult than he thought.

* * * * *

Belle Coeur had been in Jordan's family since before the Civil War. She could trace her ancestors back to the early seventeen hundreds. As she thought about selling, guilt and regret tugged at her heart. But what choice did she have? This home, this land, had been someone else's dream. Weren't her dreams equally important?

The large white house had always felt like a cozy little home to Jordan, despite its overwhelming size. Standing at the end of the long paved road leading to the house, Jordan's attention was drawn to the imposing structure. Tall Doric columns on either side of the front porch steps seemed to stretch to the sky and support the roof without effort. Grandma's always well-manicured geraniums overflowed from the handcrafted whitewashed window boxes as well as from plastic green pots scattered around the porch.

"Rot has settled in here and these boards will need to be replaced," Sam pointed out as they headed toward the house and walked up the front porch steps. "The entire exterior needs to be scraped and repainted."

Flakes of paint glared at Jordan from the wooden clapboards on the front of the house, giving silent testimony to the weathering of the years. Despite the deterioration, the house's beauty remained.

At least in her eyes. To a prospective buyer, they'd see old and in need of repair. To her, it was home.

No. It wasn't home. Home had been Grandma, and Grandma was gone now.

Home was New York.

Jordan agreed with Sam's assessments of the outside. She knew it was bad. Grandma had been an impeccable housekeeper, but there wasn't much an old woman living alone could do about the exterior of the house or big projects that needed to be tackled.

Fortunately the lawn and gardens had been maintained by friends and neighbors who routinely came to mow, trim the trees and hedges and pull a few weeds. The lush beauty of the landscape remained, the tall cypress trees bending over the long drive leading up the house, as if extending welcome to visitors. Azaleas and camellias lined the driveway and front of the house, showing their bright colors every spring.

Sam handed Jordan his clipboard and retrieved an extension ladder from his truck. He quickly ascended to the roof, and she was amazed at his surefootedness. Like a cat, all muscle, sinew and grace. The mere act of watching him move set her heart fluttering and her hormones into overdrive. Desire flared sharp and sudden, pebbling her nipples and making her wet.

She *never* got hot just looking at a guy. What the hell was wrong with her?

Stop acting like a teenager for God's sake. He's only walking on the roof, not doing a striptease. Although the thought of Sam stripping naked on the roof of Belle Coeur made her giggle. Good thing he couldn't hear her.

"The entire roof needs to be replaced," he said on his way down the ladder.

No, she would *not* watch his firm ass as he descended.

"My guess is you've got some water leaks inside because there are more than a handful of shingles missing. We'll take a look at the walls and ceilings when we go in."

Once inside, they did find some water damage. The worst areas were in the great room, the largest room in the house. Jordan always envisioned this room as the place where cotillions were held during the antebellum days. She remembered standing in the middle of the room as a child, twirling around in circles as if she were dancing in a hoop dress, a southern beau at her side.

Over the years the emptiness of the room had been replaced by more and more furniture until the great room was more of a living area. Two oversized sofas and high-back chairs were positioned directly in front of the fireplace for reading and warmth in the wintertime. Large wool rugs covered the hardwood floors. Tall, built-in bookcases lined either side of the fireplace and were filled with old volumes of literary classics. There were books predating the Civil War, and several more that were likely worth a small fortune.

She'd have to go through all the books. Selling the house was one thing. She hadn't thought about what she'd do with the furniture and other items, most of which had been here as long as the house itself. Some she'd want to keep, and the rest she'd either sell off at an auction or give away to Grandma's friends.

That ache in the pit of her stomach hit again as she thought about selling anything in the house. It would be like selling off her family's history—more importantly, Grandma's history. But what would she do with all the things here if she didn't sell them? Her apartment in New York was a cracker box, barely big enough for all her personal things, let alone the extensive collections of books and antiques littered throughout this huge, rambling home.

"This room needs the most work."

Feeling utterly miserable, she nodded at Sam's assessment and followed as he pointed out the areas where the water damage was the worst.

"Look here." Sam stopped her as she was leading him upstairs. "The banister is loose. Could be rot or maybe just needs adjustment."

"Really. I hadn't noticed that before." When she leaned over to examine the rail more closely, she heard Sam's sharp intake of breath behind her and half-turned. His eyes were hot and dark, his gaze assessing her hungrily. The stairway suddenly seemed very confined and quite warm. The heat of her blush warmed her face.

How old was she, anyway? It wasn't like this was the first time a man had ogled her.

Of course, ten years ago she'd have given up a kidney to have Sam look at her the way he was right now.

Quickly turning away, she hurried up to the second floor. Before she did something really stupid, like leap on him right there on the stairway.

Ignoring the building heat between her legs, she followed him from room to room, saying nothing while he made notes.

"The three smaller bedrooms are fine. No water leakage so I'll just recommend repainting them," Sam said as he continued to make notes while heading down the hall to the master bedroom.

They entered Jordan's bedroom, formerly her grandmother's. She loved this room, with its fireplace tucked neatly into the far corner wall. A tapestry-covered loveseat sat in front of the fireplace. Grandma used to read to her as they both snuggled under quilts in front of a warm fire on cold winter nights.

A large cherry four-poster bed sat against the opposite wall. Grandma's handmade blue and white wedding ring quilt adorned the bed, along with several matching decorative pillows. Sam looked around, then sat down on the edge of her bed and made more notes.

Except for that hot glance on the stairs, he had been completely businesslike after breakfast. She wondered why she felt disappointed. It's not like she wanted him to notice her, flirt with or tease her, so why did she feel this way?

Watching him sitting on her bed provoked sudden unbidden thoughts. She envisioned herself next to him, her fingertips gliding over his skin. A desire to reach out and touch his muscular arms and chest overwhelmed her. Closing her eyes, she took the vision further.

Would he storm over and take what he wanted from her? Would he pull her roughly against him and ravage her mouth, forcing his tongue inside?

Yes. That's what she wanted. Take it from her, demand it. He'd pull at her clothes, not caring whether they ripped or not. In a frenzy of lust, he'd tear her panties off and bury his face between her legs.

Her cunt swelled, arousal heating her from the inside out. She fanned her face and imagined his hot tongue on her clit, licking in slow circles, driving her crazy with the need to come.

Then he'd bend her over the bed, forcing her face down into the mattress and nudging her legs apart with his knee. She'd wait, anticipation making her tremble, until the moment his hot cock plunged inside her, making her scream.

Sam wouldn't be a one-minute man, either. He'd fuck her for hours, make her beg for it, take her to the edge over and over before dragging an ear-splitting orgasm from her and then following up with a roaring one of his own.

Then, when it was over, he'd take her again. In her ass this time, powering his thick cock inside her anus and forcing her to slide her fingers inside her pussy until she came again and again and—

Good lord where did that come from? Her eyes flew open and met Sam's at the same time she was trying to shake off thoughts of hot, animal sex with him. As if he'd read her mind, his lids half closed and his lips curled in a smile that could only be described as earth-shatteringly sexy. Only this time he wasn't smirking. He stared at her boldly, assessing her reaction. Jordan returned the look, unable to avert her eyes as some invisible link between them held her gaze on his.

Her body was hot, aroused, primed for sex. Did he know that? Could he sense her need? What would she do if her fantasy became reality?

The room seemed to shrink as they remained focused on each other. A flush crept up her body. Her pulse quickened, and her lips parted as her breathing grew erratic. Sam's gaze pinned her, held her in some kind of time warp where they were the only two people who existed, the only thing that mattered.

As if exposed to a sudden chill, her nipples hardened without benefit of touch. Thoughts of what she and Sam could do in that bed continued to flood her mind. Sam's hot, promising looks further fueled her mental fires.

With lightning speed he bridged the distance between them. Jordan knew she should move away, make some light conversation, do something. Anything but just stand there. But she couldn't. For some reason her feet wouldn't move.

His eyes raked boldly over her, sliding down her body like a caress. She felt each glance as if he were touching her. When he reached out and pulled gently on a long red curl that had escaped her ponytail, she couldn't hold back her gasp. Not breaking eye contact, he rubbed the curl between his fingers. She shivered in response to the light tug. Such a simple gesture and yet so erotic.

Oh God, he was going to kiss her. His full lips were only inches from hers. Jordan had to stop him now because she wasn't sure she'd be able to if he placed his mouth on hers. Summoning up what little remaining inner strength she had, she stammered out, "Sh…should we go into the bathroom?"

Sam paused. His warm breath caressed her face as he responded with, "Huh?"

"The…the bathroom. I thought you might want to see if any repairs were needed in there."

Sam cocked his head to the side as if he was trying to decipher a foreign language. Then, the light in his eyes went out. Taking a deep breath, he backed away and retrieved the clipboard from her bed.

"Sure. The bathroom. Let's go have a look."

Jordan let out the breath she had been holding, and willed her heart to beat normally. Inhaling to clear her head, she followed Sam into the bathroom.

But he was already on his way out. "I think I have it all. I'll go downstairs and come up with some numbers for you, then we can discuss it." He turned without another look at her and headed out the door.

Exhaling the breath she hadn't been aware she'd been holding, she sat on the edge of the tub and took a minute to calm down. She had grossly underestimated her attraction to Sam. At first she had chalked it up to a reminiscence of her first crush come to life again. But now she could see that whatever she felt for him when she was sixteen was nothing in comparison to what was going on inside her now.

This couldn't happen. She did not want to have feelings for someone like Sam Tanner. He didn't fit into her plans at all, and she wasn't about to fall for someone like him, someone who oozed charisma and sexuality.

Once he gave her his bid and sent someone to do the repairs, she would have no contact with him. In fact, now would be a good time to start. Jordan couldn't wait to get him out of her house.

Determined to finalize things as quickly as possible, she headed downstairs, hoping he had the numbers worked up for the cost of repairs.

She found him at the kitchen table with his clipboard and calculator.

"Okay, I think I have it." Gone were the hot glances he had exchanged with her earlier, replaced by an impersonal look. "Here's what I came up with. This includes both material and labor, and I think it's a fair price for what needs to be done." He pushed the clipboard towards her.

The amount did seem fair. Jordan wasn't sure how he could make a profit at this price, but she figured he must know what he was doing.

"Money's kind of tight for me right now, but I shouldn't have any difficulty paying you once the house is sold." Wondering how she'd be able to advance him funds, she asked, "Do you need anything up front?"

He gathered his things and rose from the table. "No, that's not necessary. You can pay in one lump sum after the job is done and the house is sold. I'll have a contract drawn up and sent over this afternoon for your signature."

"Fine. When will you send a crew to get started?" Jordan couldn't wait to get him out of her life, out of her house, and out of her thoughts. The sooner the work was done, the quicker she'd get back to her life in New York.

You're running.

She was not. And that little voice inside her head was beginning to piss her off.

"No crew. My men are all busy working on the new mall in town. However, it just so happens I have some free time, and seeing how much I've always liked this house, I'm going to take personal charge of the project and do it myself."

"What?" Did he just say what she thought he did?

"I'll be here bright and early tomorrow morning. I'll let myself out," he said and headed down the hall. Jordan heard the door close behind him as he left.

This couldn't be happening. He couldn't do this to her. She'd have to put up with seeing him, having him around, all day, every day until the work was done. Considering what had just happened upstairs, she wasn't sure her willpower was strong enough to withstand the temptation of Sam Tanner.

Now what? She couldn't very well sit around all day and look at him. That would drive her crazy. Already her nerve endings were raw from the exchange upstairs, and that was just a look. If she had to endure it every day…

She needed something to do. But what?

Maybe tomorrow she'd head into town and find some books at the library, or some project to work on, or possibly catch up with some of her old friends. Anything to put some distance between her and Sam.

Chapter Three

What was it with that man's timing? Jordan raced downstairs wearing only a short bathrobe, still dripping wet from the shower she had barely stepped out of when the blasted doorbell started ringing.

She threw open the door to give Sam a piece of her mind, and was dumbstruck at the sight of him in his tattered old gym shorts and sleeveless muscle shirt. How could a man so incredibly irritating have the ability to spark a desire in her to grab him by the shirt and plant a hot, wet kiss on his full, sexy lips?

"Damn, Jordan." Those incredible eyes raked over her half-clad body. "You sure know how to answer the door in the morning. Yesterday the sexy T-shirt, today this tiny robe—maybe tomorrow morning you could answer the door naked."

She tapped her wet foot on the foyer floor and gathered the folds of her bathrobe around her. "Look, Sam. I'm in a hurry this morning, I'm obviously soaking wet, and I really wish you wouldn't lean on my doorbell every time you come over. Can't you just start working without having to announce your presence?"

He grinned and stepped inside. "Well, I suppose I could do that, but then again I thought you wouldn't mind if I brewed some coffee before I started. Besides, I can't resist these early morning views of you."

Which was entirely bullshit. He just wanted to irritate her, and was succeeding.

"You're all wet. Why don't you go get dressed and I'll get us some coffee?" He headed into the kitchen, leaving Jordan standing in a puddle of water.

She mumbled under her breath as she stomped furiously up the stairs. "I'm pretty sure this is my house, dammit. Didn't know I had a roommate now, telling me what to do, making himself at home as if he lived here."

The nerve of the man. Apparently he had no manners whatsoever. Did he barge into everyone's homes whenever he was hungry for breakfast and wanted a cup of coffee? Or did he only delight in irritating her?

Grabbing some clothes to put on, she hurriedly combed her hair and headed downstairs to see about getting her unwelcome guest out of her kitchen.

Coffee was already brewing and the cups and cream were on the table when she entered the kitchen. He looked up and smiled. "I'm disappointed. You have clothes on."

Ignoring his comment, she asked, "What are your plans for today?"

"Thought I'd get started outside," he replied as he poured coffee. "I plan on stripping some of the paint off the house, pulling off a few of the boards and replacing them so I can start painting."

She took the coffee he offered, mumbling her thanks as she sipped the steaming brew. "I still don't understand why you're doing this work yourself. Surely you have some laborers who can do it for you?"

"I don't mind. I like to work with my hands. And I'm short-handed right now. My men are all busy with other projects, and rather than putting you off for a month or more since I know you're in a hurry, I'll just do the job myself."

"I could have waited a bit."

"Really. A month or more?"

He had her there. "Well, no, but—"

"Anyway," he added with a grin, "this job has great perks. I get to hang around a beautiful woman and get paid for it. Sure can't beat that."

"Well you're going to have to do without me today. I'm going into town and will be gone most of the day." She tried to ignore the fact he said she was beautiful.

"Being around me too much for you Jordan?"

The ego of the man astounded her. "In your dreams. I'm simply going to do some shopping." Having already had more than enough of his comments, she rose from the table and went to the sink to wash her cup. When she turned around, he was smirking at her.

"I think you just can't handle being near me."

Refusing to be baited, she replied, "And I think you just can't handle that a woman wouldn't want you."

His movements were slow and deliberate as he headed in her direction. He leaned against the counter, his hip brushing hers. The sensation of having his body touching hers was unnerving. Jordan felt the heat flowing between them, and looked up to object. His face was inches from hers.

He spoke in a near whisper as he moved in closer. "Oh, I think I could handle it if a woman didn't want me. But that's not the case here, is it?"

When his voice caressed her like that, she couldn't think straight. He was deliberately trying to confuse her, trying to draw a response. A response she wasn't ready, or willing, to give.

"I don't want you, Sam," she lied, dipping her head down to stare at her feet, unable to meet his gaze.

Absently reaching for one of her long curls, he said, "I think I scare you, Jordan. I think when I get close to you like this, you feel something, and that scares the hell out of you—makes you want to run."

You're running.

Dammit, the conversation was heading in a direction she didn't want to go. She placed her coffee cup on the counter and pressed her hands against Sam's chest to move him out of her way. But for some inexplicable reason she left them resting on his chest, exerting no pressure to push him back. She could feel his heart beating beneath her palm, his chest rising and falling. Like her own, Sam's heart beat rapidly, his breathing quickened, and Jordan knew that he was as affected by their contact as she. What would happen if she leaned closer instead of moving away?

Disaster, that's what.

"I'm not running, and I'm not afraid of you. I just don't want to do this," she said to his chest, not wanting to look up into those deep blue pools. Fearing what she might see or do if she looked in his eyes, she kept her gaze fixed below his face.

"Why not?" He breathed into her hair and lazily ran his fingers up and down the middle of her back. Despite the heat of the morning, she shivered. His erection was unmistakable as he leaned lightly against her hip. Jordan found the fact so incredibly erotic it made her legs weak.

Her blood was pounding in her ears, and if she didn't get away from him she'd do something she'd regret.

The realization hit her, effectively shutting down the heat passing between the two of them. She was weak. A sucker for a charmer, just like her mother had been. And Jordan vowed a long time ago that she'd never be like her mother.

Her body may want him, but her mind was stronger. And her mind didn't want this at all.

"Get out of my way, Sam," she said firmly. "I don't want this."

Sam paused for a moment, his breathing erratic and his pulse still racing under her hand. Finally, he inhaled deeply and backed away enough so that Jordan could look at him. What she saw took her breath away. Hot desire was evident in the way his eyes darkened like the sky before a storm. Pulling his hand through his hair, he sighed deeply.

"Enjoy your day in town." His voice was rough as he turned away from her. "I'll be outside all day, but if you wouldn't mind leaving the door open, I can pop in here for a drink occasionally."

Her heart pinged against her ribs as she watched him walk away, her body still on fire from his touch. He made her feelings churn inside until she was completely confused. Maybe it was because she had never been around someone like Sam, had never wanted or encouraged relationships with men like him.

Certainly she'd had relationships before. And of course had sex with men before. But she'd purposely chosen men who she would never fall in love with. Men whose sexuality wasn't so potent it threatened to consume her. She had always been in control.

Until now. Sam made her feel completely and totally out of control.

Feeling the need for escape, she grabbed her purse and keys and headed into town.

* * * * *

Jordan pulled into a parking spot in front of the Magnolia Library. If she was lucky, the library might have some dramatic plays or possibly even some Shakespeare. Once she started her own theater, she planned on producing the classics, some twentieth-century dramas, and of course her favorite — musicals. Maybe even hold a class or two on acting as well as stage production.

The thought of realizing her dream caused childlike excitement within her. Jordan had wanted to own a theater for as long as she could remember. From the time she got the part of the evil queen in the seventh grade production of *Snow White*, Jordan had been hooked.

At first it was the acting, but as she got more involved during high school, Mrs. David, the drama director, taught her everything else. She learned set design, blocking, lighting, everything there was to know about putting on a play. She was even allowed to produce and direct the senior play.

Her first stop when she entered the library was the information desk. Not a huge library, there was only one person at the desk to provide information as well as handle book returns and checkouts.

The woman at the desk spotted Jordan and erupted into a huge smile. "Why Jordan Lee, how nice to see you."

"Mrs. Cutter, how nice to see you again." Emily Cutter and her husband James owned Cutter Clothing, one of the oldest retail establishments on Main Street.

Emily was a small, thin woman with short gray hair and huge tortoiseshell glasses that overpowered her face. She had always been so sweet to Jordan when Grandma brought her to Cutter's to shop. "How are you and Mr. Cutter doing?"

"We're doing just fine, dear. James is busy as ever at the store. Always a new line coming in, you know. We've got a great sale on our western wear right now. You'll just have to stop in and see. I know Mr. Cutter would be so happy to see you. Have you moved back to Magnolia now? You know your Grandma always wanted you to come back home."

What was it about folks in this town and their ability to talk about ten different subjects in a single breath?

"Thank you, Mrs. Cutter. I'm just here for a visit. I'm going to stay for about a month to get Grandma's place repaired and ready to sell, and then I'll be on my way back to New York."

"I heard you were planning to sell Viola's place," Emily said, her face registering the sadness that Jordan felt but refused to acknowledge.

Of course, the fact that everyone knew she was selling the house didn't come as any surprise. The grapevine moved fast in a small town.

"Yes, I will be."

"That makes us all very sad. We were hoping you'd want to stay on at the house, come back here where you belong. But you young ones always have to reach for the stars, now don't you?"

Jordan laughed. "I don't know about that, Mrs. Cutter. But I'm happy in New York, and I have plans for the future. I'd like to start my own community theater, which is why I'm here. Do you have any books on dramatic works, maybe Shakespeare, or even Hemingway?"

Emily appeared lost in thought. "Community theater, huh? Well isn't that a grand idea? How exciting for you, Jordan. Of course, you wanted books. Aisle twelve, left-hand side should be where you'll find what you're looking for."

As Jordan thanked her and started to walk away, Emily added, "By the way, Jordan Lee, you might want to stop in at the Magnolia Community Theater. It's right next door and I hear they're planning to put on a production for the Summer Festival. Maybe you could give them some guidance."

Community theater? In Magnolia? Some things did change after all. There had never been a community theater here before, nor anything else cultural or theatrical other than the high school productions. Now she was intrigued. "I'll do that Mrs. Cutter. Thank you, it was wonderful to see you."

After browsing the books, she chose a few that looked promising. Wishing she'd brought her own books on production and set design, Jordan settled on a little Hemingway, Shakespeare and a few romance novels that she'd found in another aisle. Well, why not? Just because she read the classics didn't mean she couldn't get into a nice hot romance now and then. Besides, wicked sex with the man of your dreams only occurred in literary fiction.

And with vibrators and a rich fantasy life. Jordan got plenty of that and had a suitcase full of toys to play with.

Sex with a vibrator was always safer. She'd never have to get her heart broken that way, and she'd never fall for the wrong man.

Taking a seat in the reading area, she browsed the books she'd selected. But she was too restless to read. Her mind was on her theater.

Although she was sure she'd make a tidy sum of money selling Grandma's house and land. With New York real estate prices being what they were, she wouldn't be able to buy an exceptional piece of property. But she didn't care. Her dream was to have her own theater, and that dream was closer to coming true now than it had ever been.

After checking out the books, she walked outside and headed next door. A sign above the building read *Magnolia Community Theater*. When she peeked in the window she saw a group of people, some painting what appeared to be a set. The remaining group was arguing, but Jordan couldn't hear what it was about. Her curiosity piqued, she opened the door and stepped inside. All hell appeared to be breaking loose.

"Lola, you don't have a clue how to produce a play. What makes you think you can run things around here?" a man's booming voice echoed in the near-empty room.

Jordan recognized Lola Feldman, one of Magnolia's famous busybodies. A middle-aged woman with bleached blonde hair teased to unimaginable heights, Lola was always in the middle of things, and usually taking charge.

"Well!" Lola huffed. "Somebody has to do it, and I don't see any of you volunteering for the job! Frankly, I don't want it either. But I've got enough community spirit to know if someone doesn't take over, there will be no play to put on at the Summer Festival. Why, think of the disappointment of all our fans!"

A petite young woman with pixie short dark hair piped in. Jordan smiled as she recognized her old friend, Katie Grayson, the daughter of Grandma's neighbor, Millie. Katie and Jordan had played together as kids. If she'd been close to anyone in Magnolia, it had been Katie. Unfortunately, they'd lost touch over the years. Okay, it had been Jordan who'd lost touch.

Why was everything about Magnolia a bad memory? She'd had good times here.

"Fans? We have fans?" Katie looked around the room in mock curiosity. "And where might those supposed fans be? C'mon Lola, you know darn well this is our first production and we barely exist in the minds of the folks around here. Yeah, people are excited about having a theater, but that could hardly be called a fan club."

Jordan smiled when she spotted one of her other high school friends, George Lewiston. "Katie's right, Lola. But then so are you. We have a responsibility to put this show on. There's no point in having a community theater if we can't put on a production. And we've waited for this a long time. Trouble is, none of us have the experience to do it. So now what do we do?"

It was all Jordan could do not to laugh. This was typical small-town drama. She might as well speak up and let the people in the room know they had company. "Excuse me," she said softly.

Heads turned. The room wasn't large, but it was full. There must have been twenty people in there, and all eyes turned to Jordan.

Standing next to Katie was her mother, Millie Grayson. Millie was a short, plump bundle of energy. Famous for her peach pies, and one of Grandma's dearest friends.

"Jordan!" Katie squealed in delight. "How wonderful to see you!" She ran over and enveloped Jordan in a hug. "I'm so glad you're here. We've hardly had time to talk since you came back."

"I know, I've been busy." She really had been meaning to wander over and visit Katie, she'd just been...

What? Brooding? Hiding?

Running?

"Come on in," Katie said. "Maybe you can offer some advice. Have you come to help us?"

Before she could respond, Millie ran up and threw her chubby arms around Jordan, squeezing her in a cheerful hug. Jordan's face was suddenly smashed into a nest of teased brown hair held in place by at least one entire can of hairspray.

"Jordan Lee Weston! Why haven't you come to see me? I baked four pies yesterday and was hoping you'd stop by so we could chat."

Chat her foot. Millie hoped Jordan would stop by so she could grill her about Sam and every personal detail about her life. Good-natured and a wonderful woman, Millie was also the queen of Magnolia gossip.

Jordan laughed. "Sorry, Millie. I'll try to get over within the next day or so. As far as your play, I don't know what kind of help you need. Actually I just peeked my head in to see what was going on. What's the problem?"

Lola butted in with a response. "Well, this is the problem. Our former director, Betsy Daniels, has apparently up and eloped with her young fiancé, who got a job offer in Virginia, leaving us without any direction. And since Betsy was the most experienced, having taken two semesters of drama at the community college, we were trying to figure out who was going to take over this production."

Millie piped up immediately. "Jordan Lee can do it. She's the expert. She even works in the theater in New York City!"

She cringed at the oohhs and aaahs that were voiced over her theater experience. Why didn't she just cruise by the window and keep on walking?

"I'm not here for that long. But thanks for the offer." No way was she getting involved in this.

Katie pleaded. "C'mon Jordan. We'd love to have you direct our play. We're putting on a production of *The Music Man* for the Summer Festival next month. Rehearsals barely started when Betsy decided she had to get married right away. Anyway, that leaves us without a director. Please say you'll help us."

She eyed Katie suspiciously, refusing to be swayed by the batting of the baby blues. Definitely not. Jordan smiled benignly. "I really can't. I have so many things to do during the short time I'm here; I just couldn't devote enough time to your play."

The room got quiet. Crestfallen faces surrounded her, and she immediately felt a twinge of guilt.

No, no, no! She wasn't going to get roped into directing this play. She had things to do and didn't have time. Even if it was something she'd enjoy. Even if it would pass the time until she left.

Then a thought struck home. If Jordan busied herself with directing the play, she'd have less exposure to Sam. And that would almost be worth it.

"When's the Summer Festival?" she asked, hardly able to believe she'd even consider doing it.

"Next month," Katie replied. "You're reconsidering, aren't you? You never could resist me, you know."

Jordan laughed. Funny how she could so easily slip into the old routines. In fact, she would still be here then, having committed to staying for at least a month. It would be good practice for the day she'd own her own theater. And, she had to admit, The Music Man was one of her favorites.

Looking at the expectant faces in the room, she relented. "Sure, I'd love to help."

Cheers resounded in the room, and those in the room she didn't know came up to introduce themselves.

The door opened and a tall figure entered. "Am I late?"

Jordan was surprised to see Tony Darnell, Sam's partner at TNT Construction. He was apparently equally surprised to see Jordan and to find out she was their new director.

"Well that role should fit you well, shouldn't it, honey?" he said with a wink.

"What role do you play in this musical, Tony?"

"The lead, of course," he said, charming her with his boyish grin.

Jordan shook her head. It didn't surprise her that half the town would be involved in this production in one way or another. It was a mystery how people made a living around here, and still managed to do the extra things they always found time to do.

George explained, "We meet three times a week in the evening and then on Saturdays and Sundays for rehearsals. We just happened to be here today because Betsy left and we had to have an emergency meeting to figure out what to do. Must be fate that brought you to our door at this particular time, Jordan. We're sure glad you're here."

She didn't believe in fate, but she was still happy to have stumbled into an opportunity to do what she loved, even for only a short time. It would help combat boredom and would also keep her mind off Sam, where it had been lingering way too frequently since she arrived.

The rest of the day was spent with the cast and crew going over their roles. She was going to take the script and set design plan home and make some notes. Since tomorrow was Saturday, the cast was going to meet at her house to go over the script, so she had to get through it tonight.

Jordan had to admit, having people at the house would put a buffer between her and Sam, something she desperately needed. There were already getting to be too many close encounters, and although firm in her resolve, she wasn't Joan of Arc. Never having had great sex and being in such close proximity to someone she knew could probably give it to her was trouble in the making.

How sad to realize that the last great sex she'd experienced had been with one of her many vibrators.

She really needed a man.

No, she didn't, actually. Her mother had felt the need for a man in her life at all times. And when she couldn't find any in Magnolia, she'd taken off, leaving her child behind.

Jordan would never need a man so badly she'd go hunting for one.

Shaking off thoughts of men and sex, specifically one man in particular, she turned her attention back to the play. Admittedly, she was excited about producing and directing the musical, even if it was a small-town event. And when she could get back to New York and start her own theater, all her dreams would come true. She wouldn't need love, or a man, to make her happy.

Many women found fulfillment in their careers instead of a relationship. She wasn't her mother, and didn't yearn for the same things her mother had. Jordan was content to have her work. She didn't need love, and she definitely didn't need Sam Tanner.

Chapter Four

Jordan was busily thinking of production notes, scenery and set design when she pulled into the drive in front of her house.

Mounds of paperwork threatened to topple out of her arms as she struggled her way up the porch steps. She didn't notice Sam standing with his back to her in front of the door until she ran right into him, dropping everything she was holding.

"Whoa. You driving the bus that just ran over me?" He steadied her with his hands, and as she bent down to retrieve her papers knelt beside her to help.

"I'm…I'm sorry," she stammered. "I was thinking of something else and trying to juggle these papers and I didn't even see you there. God, what a mess," she said, looking at the jumbled pile of papers covering the front porch. A slight breeze was blowing and some of the papers were scattering off the porch and into the yard. "Oh no, I have to get those!"

"Don't worry, I'll help you round those up." The two of them set off running after papers like a couple of butterfly hunters, no more getting close to one than a gust of wind would pick it up and blow it ten feet further away than it was before. They laughed as they chased papers around the front yard like a couple of kids.

When they finally had everything picked up, they collapsed on the front porch swing and Sam helped her organize the mess. They were both out of breath and still laughing.

Sam took one of the papers he had picked up and glanced at it. "Production notes?"

Jordan smiled. "Yes, I seem to have stumbled into a part-time job. I'm going to direct the musical for the summer festival."

"Guess your arrival was good timing, then. Tony told me that Betsy had run off and they were searching for a new director."

"Well I guess that's me, then."

His expression grew serious. "Jordan, this new community theater is a big deal to the people of Magnolia. Don't take it lightly just because it isn't Broadway."

The comment hurt more than she wanted to admit. "Just because I live in a large city doesn't mean I can't appreciate a small-town production. I grew up here, Sam. I know how important the small things are when you aren't given the opportunity to be exposed to the big things."

Sam held up his hands. "Hey, don't get your panties in a bunch. I was just stating a fact. You don't like small towns or anything that goes with them. Just didn't think you'd want to waste your time on a meaningless production like the one Magnolia is putting on."

Maybe she hadn't wanted to get involved in the beginning, but the idea had become more and more appealing as the day wore on. But did she project that kind of attitude toward the town? Like she thought what happened here was beneath her? "I don't think it's meaningless at all. Is that how you see me?"

Responding with a nonchalant shrug, he said, "I can only tell you my own impressions. Don't really know what everyone else thinks."

She pushed back the gnawing hurt growling in her stomach. "How dare you assume to know anything about me? Who are you to pass judgment? We hardly know each other."

"Did I hit a sore spot? Maybe you're revealing more about your true nature than you'd like to."

Her idea was to reveal nothing. Just hang in Magnolia long enough to get the house sold, and then get out. No attachments, no friendships, nothing.

"I'm not revealing anything." Her irritation grew at the thought he would make up his mind about who she was and what she thought without ever really knowing her.

"That's your problem, Jordan. You don't let anyone in, so people make up their own stories. Lots of folks have their opinions about you, about why you left town and didn't come back. Most think it's because you were looking for glitz and glamour. Sure can't find that in a place like Magnolia."

"Glitz and glamour my ass," she replied, angry at the typical small-town mindset. "Most folks don't want to know anything about me. The busybodies and gossips make up their own stories about me, just like they did about my mother, and just like they did about you. They think what they want to think, what's juicy and dirty and scandalous, not what's true."

A smile curved his bottom lip. "What stories about me? Now you've got me curious. Were they good ones?"

It figured Sam wasn't the least bit concerned about any gossip spread about him. Men labeled as bad boys or from the wrong side of the tracks looked on it as a badge of honor, not a criticism. Women were called trash for doing the same things that men did.

Narrow-minded double standard. Another reason she hated living here.

"So? What have you heard about me?"

She shook her head, fighting a smile at his interest. "They just said you got into some trouble and had to leave town. Nothing specific, just enough to get the town gossips' curiosity going, and the grapevine took care of the rest."

"Like what?"

"I'd heard you had been arrested for drug dealing. Another story said you were involved in organized crime, and had to go into the Witness Protection program because you were testifying against a mob boss."

Sam paused, then threw back his head and laughed out loud. "No shit? Witness Protection?" His laughter rolled on until Jordan couldn't help but let her smile run free.

"Well? Is any of it true?"

He choked out a last chuckle and shook his head. "Nope."

"See what I mean? Typically, gossip is not rooted in fact at all, but fantasy. Most people don't really know anything about me, or why I left or what I've been doing."

"Then tell me."

The seriousness of his statement unnerved her. "Tell you what?"

"Tell me about you, Jordan. I'd like to know why you left, what you've been doing, what your dreams are."

"Why would you be interested?" she blurted, wishing immediately that she hadn't.

"Because I'm interested in you. I want to know about you." A soft breeze whipped a curl across her cheek, and Sam swept it away with his fingertips.

She shivered at the contact.

"Interested how?"

He smiled. "You can take the frightened bunny look out of your eyes. Not *that* kind of interested."

Jordan relaxed. Then paused a moment to think. Suddenly she wondered why Sam wasn't "that kind of interested". What was wrong with her? She wasn't repulsive, could carry on a decent conversation and occasionally even showed a sense of humor. So why wasn't Sam interested in her? In *that* way.

"Why not?"

Sam looked confused. "Why not what?"

"Why aren't you interested in me *that* way?"

"In what way?"

"Sam! You know what way I'm referring to. Stop confusing me."

"I'm confusing you? Are you sure it's not the other way around?"

"Answer my question!" Geez, the man was frustrating.

"What question?"

"Oh my God you are so dense! You know the question!"

He laughed then, and when she thought about it for a second, she did too.

"Seriously, I am interested. In knowing everything about you. You intrigue me, and sometimes you confuse me, but I'm still interested."

"Confuse you about what?"

"About your reasons for leaving this town. I've been where you are. Thinking I could find my life outside of Magnolia. It didn't work for me. I'm curious how it's working for you."

His turquoise gaze was probing and curious, and also much too hot and sexy for her liking.

Is this what her mother experienced? The desire to have a man show interest in her, someone to care about what she did? She wanted to tell him, wanted him to know about her. And she wanted to know about him. But finding out about Sam Tanner would mean she cared about him, and she most certainly did not. She wouldn't allow herself to.

She was too comfortable. Sitting next to Sam on the porch swing felt natural, as if they'd been doing it for years. The longer she sat and talked with him, the more she'd want to know about him, want him to know about her. The more she'd come to just purely want him in the physical sense.

All were dangerous. They signaled interest in a relationship. The way her body had been feeling lately, so in tune to him, she knew it only meant trouble. It was time to escape.

"I'd love to sit around here all day and talk about me, me, me, but I have things to do." She rose and gathered her papers, looking down at Sam, who continued to leisurely swing. "And am I not paying you to do something around here, or do you just intend to take up my time and do nothing?"

"Why don't you take a look at what I've done, and then tell me if you feel like you're getting your money's worth."

When she first got home all the papers had scattered, so she hadn't seen what Sam had done that day. Now that he pointed it out, she could see all the step and porch boards that were rotted or cracked had been replaced, the front door was painted, as was the entire porch.

He'd done a hell of a lot of work. And she hadn't been aware of any of it.

Had she noticed earlier, she would have seen the paint and dirt stains all over Sam's shirt and shorts. He was filthy, sweaty, dusty...and absolutely gorgeous. Sweat glistened off his muscular arms and shoulders, and a smudge of dirt on his cheek did nothing to detract from his classically handsome features.

Looking at him did strange things to her—created aches in areas of her body that had never ached before. And to top it all off, he had to act curious about her, wanting her to talk about herself and her life, as if he was really interested. No, she wasn't going to fall for that line.

It was best to keep things businesslike between them, no matter what her body and her heart wanted.

"Yes, I can see you did a fine job today," she replied, purposely adding a brusque tone to her voice. "Now if you'll excuse me, I've got work to do. You can just clean up your stuff and take off whenever you're done for the day." Effectively dismissing him with a turn away, she hurried inside, shutting the door quickly behind her.

Leaning against the inside of the front door, she felt shame wash over her. Shrewish behavior wasn't like her at all. Sam had worked hard on the house, and she should have noticed. Should have shown her appreciation. Instead she insulted him and his work.

What the hell was wrong with her?

Not that she needed to look far for the answer. Being around him unnerved her, made her feel things she didn't want to feel. Her only thought had been escape. To run. Just like Sam said she always did when she was around him. And he was right. She was still running.

Frustrated and angry at both Sam and herself, she ran upstairs and sat on the bed. Pent-up anxiety swirled through her, too many emotions she'd rather not recognize churning her insides out.

Relax, Jordan. Quit thinking so much.

Right. Like that would ever happen.

Only one thing was going to calm her down right now. She needed release, the kind that would only come from sex.

Since that wasn't going to happen anytime soon, she'd have to rely on her vibrators.

Nothing like whirling gizmos and jellied toys as her only way of sexual release. But at least she could think about Sam, about what could have been between them, in the safety of her own bedroom.

He'd never know that her sexual fantasies revolved around him, that she imagined him fucking her when she fucked her vibrator.

Just the thought had her pussy quivering.

With a sigh of eager anticipation, she laid on the bed and reached into her nightstand drawer.

* * * * *

Sam climbed the scaffold at the side of the house to retrieve the paint and tools, too pissed off to even think straight.

Dismissed him. She had just walked away and dismissed him.

Fine. Tomorrow he'd get a crew in here to finish the job. He was busy as hell at work and things were piling up. He didn't need this kind of shit from a woman.

Especially a woman who didn't mean a goddamned thing to him.

When he reached the scaffold platform, he grabbed for the paintbrush he'd left near the bedroom window ledge.

But when he glanced in the open window, all thoughts of making a quick escape fled from his mind.

Jordan lay across the bed on her back, a pink jelly vibrator in her hand. She'd obviously shed her clothing and slipped on a short silken robe that was the same color as her fiery hair. Her eyes were closed, her hair spread around her like a willowy flame, her lips parted and her hand gently caressing her breasts through the robe.

He hardened instantly and nearly dropped to his knees. Jordan had been the fantasy of his youth—intelligent, beautiful, cool and remote, she'd been everything he wanted and didn't think he'd ever have.

Many a night as a teen he'd jacked off with her face and budding body in his mind, imagining what it would be like to see her naked, to touch her soft skin and taste her sweet mouth.

Funny, in his reality he'd always thought her too aloof to enjoy sex.

He had a feeling he was about to be proven dead wrong about that assumption.

Jordan turned on the vibrator and pulled the bottom of her robe aside. Her position on the bed afforded him a perfect view of her pussy. A strip of red curls covered her mound, and her swollen lips were bare. Glistening juices sparkled in the light shining into the room and onto the bed.

She was hot, swollen and wet. He licked his lips, almost able to imagine her taste and wishing that he could slip in the window and bury his face in her cunt until she screamed and flooded his mouth with her sweet cream.

But he couldn't do that. As it was he already felt like a voyeur, a dirty old man about to watch a woman's most private moment. And damned if he was going to budge from his spot on the scaffold.

Instead, he palmed his throbbing cock through his shorts and watched intently as she teased her clit and pussy lips with the vibrator. It whirred softly, the only sound in the quiet room.

Until she moaned. God, he loved it when a woman made noises. His cock jerked against his palm, demanding attention. Holding onto the handrail of the scaffold, he took a look around the property.

Secluded, trees barring view of the bedroom and his location, and away from the long drive. No one could see him.

He slipped the front of his shorts down under his balls and took out his cock, squeezing it hard, once again focusing his attention on Jordan.

She'd untied the sash around the robe and let it fall to the side. He sucked in a breath at her perfect, full breasts, the nipples coral-tipped and quite prominent as she plucked them with her free hand. All the while she continued to move the vibrator over her clit.

Then she moved both hands between her legs, spread them wider, and slipped the vibrator between the pink folds of her pussy. She arched her buttocks off the bed and cried out.

"Oh yes! That's so good, Sam. Fuck me deeper."

His hand stilled on his cock. Shit. She'd called his name. She was fantasizing about him. Goddammit, that was so fucking erotic he almost blew his load right then.

Instead, he gripped the head of his dick and squeezed, wanting to prolong the sweet release.

When she came, he'd come. It may be the closest he'd ever get to having sex with Jordan.

She pulled the vibrator nearly completely out of her pussy. It was covered in her creamy juices and she used it to rub them over her. Now her lips and clit were covered in glistening moisture.

Then she did something he'd never have expected. She switched to her belly, sliding a pillow under it and raising her ass in the air. Reaching into her nightstand drawer, she pulled another phallic object out, this one smaller and thinner than the big jelly vibrator. Along with a bottle of lube, which she poured liberally over the smaller object.

Then she got up on her knees and teased her anus with the small plug.

Fucking shit! Her puckered hole was throbbing as she tormented it with lube, sliding the plug an inch inside, then pulling it out.

"Yes, Sam, like that. You know I want it in the ass, baby."

Men like him didn't faint, but for God's sake she was about to kill him. His balls were tight and ready to explode, his cock so hard he could have beat it against the steel bars of the scaffold and it wouldn't have fazed him.

When she slipped the plug all the way into her ass and grunted, then shrieked, he started pumping his shaft faster and harder. She slid her pink vibrator back in her pussy and settled down on her belly, lifting her hips up and down to simulate fucking.

She reached behind and fucked her ass with the dildo, grinding her pussy against the whirring vibrator, and driving him near the brink of insanity.

"Yes, Sam, fuck my ass. Oooh yes, just like that. Harder!"

He squeezed his cock harder, thrusting fast and furious into the tight grip of his hand, imagining how hot and tight her ass would be if it were really his cock buried to the hilt inside her.

"Oh, God, Sam, Oh God, I'm gonna come!" she cried, wailing and thrashing and lifting her ass up and down while fucking the dildo harder and faster into her anus.

Then she screamed and shuddered, her entire body quivering with spasms. Sam jettisoned his come and bit back the groan he wanted to let loose. Spurt after spurt shot over the scaffold and into the bushes below. He kept pumping, and she kept writhing until she finally collapsed onto the mattress.

He was drenched in sweat and his legs were shaking, yet he managed to lift up his shorts, grab his stuff and head down the scaffold before Jordan realized he'd been witness to her wild self-pleasure.

And wild it had been. He wasn't sure if he'd ever recover from it.

Frankly, all it had done was frustrate him even more, because now he wanted her more than ever, and was pissed off at her at the same time.

Piling his things in the truck, he drove home and grabbed a cold drink from the fridge before coming back outside to unload and clean up his work tools.

God knows he needed it. Between being utterly irritated at Jordan and at the same time completely turned on from watching her masturbate, right now he needed a cold beer, followed by an even colder shower.

Time to concentrate on something else, like his house and his tools and getting his mind wrapped around something other than long legs and sweet, creamy pussy. He looked up at the modest brick and white frame house in the heart of town that he called home. Yeah, it was small, but for now it was fine.

He crouched down to wash out his paintbrushes.

The irritation he'd felt hadn't quite dissipated despite watching Jordan's fuck-herself show. He'd worked his ass off today hoping she'd notice and appreciate the quick and efficient way he was getting the project done.

First off, she hadn't even seen what he'd accomplished. Her head was a million miles away when she'd crashed into him at the front door. She hadn't said a word about it, which really wasn't a big deal. After all, she had dropped all her papers and they were distracted running around and picking them up.

Then they'd sat on the porch swing together and talked. It had been nice. Maybe things started out kind of sketchy, but then she'd seemed to relax. Admittedly, he'd been baiting her about the play and she'd had a right to be angry with him.

It was obvious she was excited about the play, but for some reason didn't want to let him know that. Whenever he got too close she backed away or changed the subject. Especially when he talked about the two of them.

Something was there between them. He felt it and was pretty certain Jordan could too. But every time they got close, she ran. Just like the high school dance. So what was it?

Why run upstairs and fuck herself with vibrators when there was a living breathing available man who made no secret of the fact he wanted her?

He wasn't exactly repulsive. So what was her fear?

And why was she so happy in New York? What could she get there that she couldn't find in Magnolia? God knows Sam had tried living away. Traveled all over the world, but never felt comfortable until he had come home. Of course his family life had been different. His parents were still married. Magnolia was the town where his parents grew up, and where they still lived. Jordan couldn't make the same claim.

Her parents had split when she was a baby, her mother chasing after any man who would have her. Jordan had told him she'd spent most of her time with her grandmother because her mother was always gone. Her mom had finally left town with one not long after Jordan graduated high school. That kind of family life changed a person.

Still didn't explain away her fear of getting close to him.

The sound of a car pulling into the driveway thrust thoughts of Jordan to the side. Temporarily at least. Sam smiled at his parents as they got out of their car.

Fred and Lois Tanner were in their early sixties, pictures of perfect health, and every bit in love with each other today as they were when they got married over thirty-five years ago.

Both still slender, they stayed active playing golf almost every day. His mother had been a beauty when she was young. Still was, her dark hair cut in a short bob which accentuated her small face and loving brown eyes. His father was still handsome as ever, tall with a full head of silvery hair.

"Evening, son," his father said as they stopped near him. "Painting?"

"Yeah. The old Belle Coeur house."

"Ah." Fred Tanner was not a man of many words, unless something important needed to be said.

"Oh, Viola's place," his mother exclaimed, kissing him on the cheek. "How's that coming along?"

Of course his mother already knew Jordan was at Belle Coeur. She was in the grapevine loop in Magnolia, and always one of the first in on any gossip.

"Coming along fine, Mom."

"And Jordan Weston, how is she doing?"

"She's fine too, Mom." Sam waited, knowing what was coming.

"She sure is a pretty little thing."

Yep, there it was.

"Is she? I hadn't noticed."

Lois Tanner lifted a wise mother's eyebrow. "Have you been struck blind recently?"

"Nope."

"Then how could you not notice that attractive woman living in the house you're working on?"

Sam walked up and sat on the porch with his parents, wiping his wet hands with a towel.

"Quit matchmaking, Mom."

Lois feigned shock. "Me? Why I'm not doing any such thing."

He smiled at her. "You are too."

"I am not. I'm just wondering how my handsome son has blinders on when it comes to the beautiful woman who is just perfect for him."

"She's not perfect for me at all."

"Why not?"

He knew better than to have this discussion with his mother, knowing it was highly unlikely she'd see his point of view.

"For starters, she's opinionated and stubborn."

His mother laughed. "And you're not?"

Ignoring that comment, he continued. "She's rude. Insulting. Thinks I'm a hillbilly."

"I know Jordan Weston and she's never had an unkind word to say about anyone in Magnolia. And," she added, "You're rude and insulting sometimes, too. Doesn't make you a bad person."

"She hates Magnolia." There, let his mother come up with a comeback to that one.

"No she doesn't. She just isn't aware of it yet. You'll have to remind her about the good things in Magnolia. Like you, for example."

This was ridiculous. No matter how old he got, he would always be reduced to an adolescent in his mother's eyes. And obviously completely unable to care for himself, let alone find his own woman.

"You've been gossiping with Millie Grayson, haven't you? And I can just bet you two have decided to play a little Cupid with Jordan and me."

"We have not."

It was all he could do not to grin. His mother was so transparent. And he just loved her to death.

And there sat his father, rocking away on the front porch, clearly taking in everything said although he tried to appear oblivious.

"You've been divorced for quite some time now, Sam," Lois continued. "Don't you think it's time you found a nice girl and gave your father and me some grandchildren?"

Oh, good God almighty. Not *that* talk again.

"When the right woman comes along, I'll give you some grandchildren."

Lois sat for a moment, contemplating her next move. "I'm not getting any younger you know."

"You're healthier than I am."

"Okay, then *you're* not getting any younger. I'd like to have grandchildren while you're still capable of making some."

"Mom!"

Lois laughed lightly. "All right, Sam, but you know what I mean. It's time to get out there and find a woman. Get married, settle down and raise a family."

Sam listened to the same old speech his mother had been giving him for years, ever since he divorced Penny.

"I've heard this before, Mom. And I did get married. You saw what happened."

Lois wrinkled her nose. "That was Penny. She wasn't right for you, anyway."

"Neither is Jordan."

"Are you sure?" His mother's eyes were searching.

Sam didn't answer, tired of defending his opinion about Jordan. They sat on the porch for awhile and watched the kids play in the yard across the street. Sam watched his mother out of the corner of his eye. He could see the wheels turning in her sharp mind. A plot was forming. That spelled trouble. Any minute now she'd come up with another zinger about how well he and Jordan could match up. Another that he'd have to refute.

But this time, instead of his mother, it was his father who had something to add. The man of few words managed to shock the hell out of him when he said, "Sometimes son, the perfect woman is right under our noses and we don't even see her."

Later that night as Sam sat in front of the television watching a ballgame, he thought about what his father had said. The perfect woman huh? And his parents thought the perfect woman for him was Jordan Weston?

Not likely. She was the furthest thing from perfect he had ever seen.

Oh she was perfectly beautiful, all right. And perfectly desirable. But a perfect match for Sam? No way.

Unless perfect pain in the ass counted.

He just wanted her. That was his problem. He lusted after the gorgeous redhead and couldn't think straight when she was around. One look at her and his dick took over, using every brain cell he had available. No wonder he couldn't think logically.

That had to be it. His motivation was purely physical. Jordan did something to him. Made him do things he wouldn't ordinarily do. Like deciding to work on Belle Coeur. Whatever possessed him to do the repairs himself, when he had vowed to stay away from her? There were plenty of TNT laborers he could have assigned to the job, but at the last minute he'd decided to do it himself.

As if he had time for it.

So in spite of his resolve to stay away from Jordan, Sam was finding ways to be near her. She wasn't even his type. Well, physically she was, of course. But Sam wanted a small-town girl who was happy living in a small town, and didn't want to be anywhere else but by his side for the rest of her life. That certainly wasn't Jordan Weston. He'd been down that road before. Next time he picked a woman, it would be one who loved him for who he was, who didn't care where they lived as long as they were together.

Maybe if he could get her in the sack a few times he could get her out of his system. He was certain she wanted him. Hell, she'd fucked herself and fantasized about him while she did it. She felt the same way he did, so why not take it a step further?

Once he exercised his physical desire for her, he could exorcise her from his mind completely.

It was time to put the full-court press on Jordan.

Chapter Five

Jordan had a different plan for the next day. Up early, she swept through the house preparing for the cast to arrive. She was already dressed when Sam rang the doorbell at eight a.m. She smiled, wondering if he was giving her a break by showing up so late. Late by Sam's standards anyway.

She whipped open the door and smiled smugly at his look of amazement.

"Up already?"

"Obviously."

Then he grinned and turned the tables on her. "Couldn't wait another minute to see me, could you?"

Ignoring his attempts to annoy her, Jordan turned and headed toward the kitchen without another word.

He was equally surprised when they entered the kitchen and Jordan poured him a cup of coffee.

"I like this domestic side of you." He sat at the table and watched her move around the kitchen. "I can picture you fixing coffee every morning. Of course we'd need it after being up all night."

"That proposition is quite unlikely to occur." She refused to allow him to bait her this morning. She sat at the table and pored over the notes she had started earlier. Maybe if she ignored him he'd get to work and leave her alone.

"You sure about that?" He reached across the table to take her hand, his thumb rubbing gently over her fingertips, eliciting mini electric shocks of pleasure. As if he'd burned her, she quickly jerked her hand away and jumped up from the table, busying herself around the kitchen.

She was disgusted at her weakness. A mere touch of his hand and her body betrayed her. Good thing she had company coming today because she no longer trusted herself alone with him.

"What are your plans for today?" She tried to focus on anything but his body by pretending to clean something. She wanted to stay in motion, figuring a moving target was harder to hit, and she'd been hit by her desire for Sam too much already.

With one eye towards Sam and the other on her work she saw him grinning, as if he knew exactly why she was flitting around like a cornered animal looking for escape.

"Thought I'd work out back today, finish replacing some of the boards and do some painting on the back porch. That okay with you boss?"

"That'll be fine. In fact, that works great for me. I have the cast from the play coming over for a read-through, so I need you out of my way."

"You feeling the need for reinforcements, sugar?"

Arousal flared to life at his use of the endearment. Dammit, why hadn't she used her vibrator last night instead of tossing and turning and wishing Sam were in bed tossing and turning with her? "I don't know what you're talking about."

She tried her best to appear uninterested while absently running the sponge over the kitchen counter.

He approached. She retreated, as far away as she could without appearing obvious. Head down, she diligently scrubbed the imaginary dirt on the counter.

"I think you know. For one thing, you're trying to distance yourself from me physically, even resorting to cleaning that four inch square of counter for the past five minutes."

Realizing he was right, she threw the sponge in the sink and turned to face him, her hands on her hips.

"I was trying to remove a stain," she lied.

"You were not. You were trying to ignore me."

"Exactly. I'm *trying* to ignore you, but you just don't get the hint." Brushing him aside, she reached for the muffins and pastries she bought at the store and placed them on the table. "Don't you have work to do?"

"In a minute. I want to talk to you about something." His tone was serious and she stopped to look at him.

"About what?"

"About you and me."

That simple statement conjured up images. Dirty little images of sweat-soaked sheets and loud moans of pleasure.

What was wrong with her? Was she possessed or something?

She searched Sam's face for some sign, but whatever was on his mind wasn't showing there.

Dreading the answer, she couldn't help but ask the question anyway. "What about you and me?"

He took a step toward her just as the doorbell rang. She paused for a second, her question still hanging in the air. But he turned away. Whatever he wanted to talk about would have to wait. Surprisingly disappointed, she went to answer the door.

The cast had arrived en masse. Jordan placed them all in the great room and served coffee and pastries. They started going over production notes and discussing the characters.

The meeting hadn't gotten very far when Sam popped in the room to say hello.

Watching him converse with everyone, she was struck by how comfortable he seemed. Laughing easily, he spoke with them about their lives and families, teased them and was teased in return. And they treated Sam with warmth and affection.

Like family.

She felt a twinge of jealousy and regret, then quickly forced the feeling away. She had made her choices. She liked New York and the feeling of anonymity it gave her. People just didn't allow themselves to bond with anyone there. Well maybe some did, but she didn't. That had never bothered her before. Why did it now?

"I know you're all busy, and my boss here is a slave driver and will dock my pay if I don't get to work, so I'd better get to it."

As he turned to leave he glanced in Jordan's direction and their eyes met. His gaze settled over her for what she thought was way too long, causing her to heat in embarrassment. But instead of averting her gaze like she should have, she stayed locked in some sort of visual foreplay with him. Surely everyone else saw the same thing Jordan saw—Sam's smoldering, hot look burning her to the spot. Then he winked and left the room.

Her gaze lingered on the now empty doorway, both longing and irritation steaming inside her. How could he do this to her? Humiliate her like this in front of people whose respect she was trying to earn? Now everyone probably thought they were having a hot love affair.

Turning her attention to the group, she was appalled to find them all staring at her, huge grins on their faces. She could imagine the thoughts going through their minds. The steamy, longing looks she and Sam had exchanged would lead anyone to believe the two of them were lovers. And in a town such as Magnolia, any fodder for the gossip mill was not a good thing. She could hear the phone lines already burning up with rumors.

Dammit!

Clearing her throat, Jordan tried to focus everyone on the play and away from her and Sam. "Okay, now where were we?"

After a couple hours of rehearsal, they took a break and grabbed some drinks, giving Jordan a chance to mentally review the first part of the day. The read-through went quite well. Surprisingly, it was a very talented group. She hadn't yet heard their singing voices, but had to admit they all had their parts down to a tee, and seemed to have a knack for bringing out the nuances of each character. She couldn't wait to hear them sing, individually and as a group.

It seemed like almost everyone had gathered in the kitchen. Tony had gone outside to speak to Sam. Millie and Katie were looking out the back window at the two men talking.

"Isn't Sam just wonderful?" Millie mentioned to no one in particular, but obviously loud enough for Jordan to hear. "Here he is, busy as can be with his business, and he takes time out to work on Viola's place. That's so typical of him. Always pitching in to help friends and neighbors."

A regular Good Samaritan, wasn't he?

"Oh, I so agree with you," piped in Lola. "Why just last month our roof sprung a leak during that terrible rainstorm, and not only did Sam send a crew over immediately, but he climbed up there himself in the middle of the pounding rain to make sure it was done right. Why, he could have been struck by lightning doing that, yet he didn't think a thing of it. He told me that he couldn't very well let a friend sit knee-deep in water, so he just did what needed to be done. Said it was no big deal."

Right. I'll bet he walks on water too.

Even Katie had to sing his praises. "Well, he's always helping folks around here without a thought to himself. He's just a really nice guy."

Jordan rolled her eyes, making a mental note to strangle Katie later.

One couldn't accuse these people of being subtle. She wondered when they'd get to the part where they described how lonely Sam was.

"Sam seems so lonely since he and Penny got that divorce," Katie said.

Bingo.

"I know he does, honey," Millie added. "He tried his best with that woman, and she never appreciated a single thing he did. All she ever thought about was herself. Personally, I was happy when the marriage ended. They just weren't right for each other."

Now comes the part where he needs a woman in his life.

"Yeah," added Millie. "That man needs a woman, for sure. He has a big heart, and needs someone he can give all his love to, who will love him in return."

If she could bottle this bullshit, Jordan would be a millionaire.

Sighing, Millie added, "And a fine specimen of a man he is. If I was thirty years younger I'd be chasing him all through town, like some of those girls here do. He never seems interested in any of them, though." Glancing in Jordan's direction, she added, "Maybe he hasn't found the right one to let catch him. Yet."

Admittedly it was a pretty good effort. And it *was* interesting to hear what everyone thought of Sam. He had a good reputation as a hard worker and a good friend and neighbor, which was quite a testimonial. She supposed she hadn't really considered Sam's good qualities, because he had the annoying habit of pissing her off on a regular basis.

Sidling over to Jordan, Katie asked, "Okay, tell me. How long have you and Sam been dating?"

It was only a matter of time before that rumor got started. "We're not, and you know that."

Glaring at her friend had no effect whatsoever. Katie wasn't the least bit intimidated. Instead, she arched her brows in surprise. "Damn, girl, if you're not, then you should be. He's hotter than a Carolina summer, if you ask me."

She didn't recall asking.

Nevertheless, Katie was intent on giving one hundred percent to her sales pitch. Wiping her brow and launching into her best southern belle impression, Katie said "Well lordy me, if I were you, I'd be askin' that hot young Sam Tanner to call on me." She concluded by fanning herself with her notes.

Jordan laughed, finally giving up and allowing herself to relax a bit.

Deciding to play along with the southern bit, she stood and said, "Why Miss Katie, surely you don't mean to say that nice-looking Mr. Tanner is available? Well my goodness me, the thought of taking up with the likes of that gentleman is enough to make a girl swoon with desire."

They looked at each other and Katie smirked. That was all it took. They both broke into a fit of laughter, only to be interrupted by a husky male voice behind them.

"Swoon with desire, Jordan? Well I had no idea you felt that way about me," Sam replied with a wicked grin as he stood in the doorway to the kitchen.

Jordan stood rooted to the spot, flames of embarrassment heating her cheeks. Then, as if things couldn't get any worse, he grabbed her and bent her backward over his left arm.

Her breath caught as he lowered his head to hers. Their eyes met, long enough for Jordan to see the turquoise orbs darken with desire. Before she could object, Sam's lips grazed hers in a soft, gentle kiss.

Without any time for thought, Jordan's instincts kicked in and her lips parted for him. He fit his mouth firmly over hers, and any further consideration of time and place went right out the window.

She sighed at the pleasure of being held in a man's arms. He tasted like coffee and peppermint, his lips sliding magically over hers. His tongue lightly teased hers, sending little shocks of awareness and desire coursing through her body. Then as quickly as it began it was over, and he pulled her upright and stood next to her, grinning.

Their performance elicited hoots, hollers and applause from everyone in the kitchen. Reality returned and Jordan realized what she had done.

She was mortified Sam had caught her playacting with Katie, especially considering he was the subject of their amusement. But then to be swooped over in his arms like that, and have him kiss her in front of all these people. She was certain the rumor mill would be running nonstop from now until Christmas. Yet despite her mortification, the taste of his kiss still burned on her lips.

How was she supposed to react to this? Should she be angry with Sam for kissing her in front of all these people? She wasn't a teenager anymore, and really shouldn't have been as affected by that brief touch of lips as she had been. It was just for fun, at least that's how it appeared to everyone else.

She'd just make the best of it and have it appear as if their little kissing scene was nothing more than a game. Jordan grabbed Sam's hand for balance and then dropped a curtsey to her audience. Sam, following her lead, bowed to their applause.

"That was so much fun!" Katie exclaimed as she ran over and hugged Jordan. "You're such a talented actress. And Sam," she said as she punched him in the arm, "Why aren't you in this play with us? You've got the romantic leading man part down, that's for certain."

Sam laughed. "I think I'll stick to where my true talents are."

"Well!" said Millie emphatically. "If you two aren't the most romantic couple since Scarlett and Rhett, I don't know who is. How long have you been dating, and why didn't I know about it?"

"We're not..." Jordan was about to correct Millie's assumption, but Sam interrupted her.

"To be honest, we haven't dated—yet. However, I was going to ask Jordan to go out with me tonight. Think my impromptu performance here could win me a date with the town's newest drama director?"

Damn, damn, damn! A glance at their audience told her there was no way she could turn him down now. Of course they expected her to say yes. According to all of these people, the two of them were a match made in heaven. Jordan would come off as hurtful and insulting if she turned him down in front of this crowd. And she bet Sam knew that too.

With a tight smile on her face she turned to Sam. "Of course. I'd love to go out with you tonight."

"Great!" he said, and another round of applause circled the room. "Pick you up here about seven-thirty. Back to work for me. I have to finish up early so I can get ready for my date." He winked at everyone, then stepped through the back door, annoying Jordan even more as he whistled his way out.

Bastard. He probably planned that whole thing just to get her to agree to a date. She'd bet Katie was in on it, too.

The Katie who was currently doing her best to avoid getting caught alone with Jordan.

Oh, she'd have words with her alleged friend later.

Heaving a great sigh of exasperation, she gathered the cast members and shuffled them back into the great room to continue their rehearsal.

A date. She couldn't believe it. As hard as she had tried to put some distance between her and Sam, her whole plan had backfired.

Looking to the heavens for divine intervention, and seeing none forthcoming, Jordan resigned herself to going out with Sam Tanner that evening.

Chapter Six

"It's not a date." Jordan glared at Katie, who'd lingered after rehearsal to "help" her get ready.

Like she needed help. Besides, it wasn't a date. As she tried to figure out what to wear she kept reminding herself of that fact.

"Is too a date." Katie sat on Jordan's bed, a bag of potato chips in one hand and a glass of iced tea in the other.

"This is your fault, anyway." Katie's and everyone else who put her up to this. Still irritated at Sam and, for that matter, the rest of the people who conned her into going out with him tonight, she hadn't planned on dressing up. She hadn't planned anything other than trying to get through the night without screaming in frustration.

"If it's not a date, how come you've tried on six different outfits in the past half-hour?" Katie asked.

Jordan did the only thing she could think of in response. She stuck her tongue out.

Katie laughed. "See? Look at that dress you're wearing. You're gonna knock him dead with that little slip of a thing. Therefore, it's a date."

"Look. The only reason I chose the yellow silk sundress is because it's so hot and humid outside."

"Uh-huh. Has nothing to do with the fact the dress rides dangerously near your upper thighs, nor that it slides over your body like lapping ocean waves. After all, you're not dressing for anyone in particular, right?"

Jordan rolled her eyes. "I can't believe I ever considered you my friend. You're supposed to be on my side."

"I am, honey. And I can feel the tension between you and Sam. Hell, everyone in town can feel it. That first love never dies, Jordie, you should know that."

"I'm not in love with Sam. Never was. It was a teenage crush, and that's all."

Shaking her head, Katie slipped off the bed and grabbed Jordan's hands. "It's okay to let someone love you. It's okay to let yourself experience it, too. You're not your mom, Jordan. Nothing like her."

And she never would be. "I'm just doing this to placate all of you. Quit making a big deal out of it. And by the way, how's your love life?"

Katie's eyes widened. "Me? I'm busy. Don't have time."

"You weren't too busy to get involved in the play. And you aren't too busy to be pushing me toward Sam. So what's going on with you?"

"Nothing."

Katie averted her gaze and stared into the bag of chips.

Hmm, definitely something up there. "Want to talk about it?"

"Nope. Nothing to talk about. My business is going well, I spend a lot of my time welding artwork, and Mom keeps up the store."

"I love those knickknacks and garden items you sculpt." Katie was a whiz at it, and had used her talents to make metalwork that sold like hotcakes at her mother's antique store.

"Thanks. Like I said, it keeps me busy."

"Too busy to find the man of your dreams?"

Katie snorted and grabbed the chips and tea. "I don't have time to dream. I'll let myself out. Enjoy your date. I want a full report tomorrow morning."

Nice evasion tactic, but Jordan would definitely be probing more into her friend's lack of social life. Hell, turnabout was fair play, right?

Jordan leaned her face into the small fan on top of the dressing table. It was hot outside, that's why she was perspiring. Not because she had exerted herself for the past half hour trying on clothes in an effort to find the right thing to wear for her non-date.

Okay, maybe the dress was short, sinfully sexy and hugged her body like a lover would. It was just a little bit possible she wanted to make Sam suffer. After all, she was frustrated at this whole charade. It was only fair that Sam put up with a bit too.

Staring at her reflection in the mirror above the dresser, Jordan barely recognized herself. Her hair fell in soft waves over her shoulders. Her face was flushed and her eyes were accented with pale gold shadow and a light coating of mascara, making them sparkle like gems. There was a glow to her skin that hadn't been there before.

Probably the heat.

Damn Katie for making her go through this. She'd have just tossed on jeans and worn no makeup, then braided her hair. But no. Katie had insisted that Sam might be taking her to a nice restaurant and she should dress accordingly.

But she not only looked different, she felt different. It couldn't be her date with Sam. She had dated plenty in New York, admittedly with men who didn't stir her senses like Sam. There was a good reason she chose stuffy business types or someone involved with theater as dates. Neither of those types of men evoked one ounce of the fire that Sam flamed within her.

There was just something about a man who worked outside, with his hands, in the heat. A man who wasn't afraid to get dirty. A man who wore jeans that hugged his body so sinfully they should be outlawed.

How could her complete aversion to men like Sam turn into an undeniable attraction that threatened to consume her every thought? And, more importantly, what was she going to do about it? Why was she dressed this way, when she knew what Sam's reaction would be? Was she doing it to aggravate him, dangle the carrot only to snatch it away when he wanted it the most? Or was she deliberately trying to attract him, make him desire her like no man ever had?

Some questions were better left unanswered.

After slipping on her sandals, she headed downstairs to wait, vowing to endure the evening like a good sport. After all, it was nothing more than dinner and then her obligation to Sam and the people who encouraged this date would be fulfilled. Then she could go about her business and he could go about his.

In a few weeks, she'd be gone. No sense in getting something started.

She glanced longingly up the stairs, wishing she'd had time to take the edge off with one of her vibrators. Her nerve endings sang in anticipation.

Anticipation of what? Nothing was going to happen tonight!

And it *wasn't* a date!

The chime of the doorbell indicated Sam was, as usual, right on time. Taking a deep breath, she opened the door.

He had brought her flowers. God, and he looked so good. Jeans again. Dark, newer than his work jeans, and of course they had to fit him perfectly, had to outline his muscular thighs, had to showcase the bulge in his crotch.

Shit.

The dark blue of his short-sleeved polo shirt accentuated his turquoise eyes. And he smelled like… Jordan inhaled. Obsession. Her favorite men's cologne. Well that figured. He looked good, smelled great, and he brought flowers. Damn him!

"Come in." She moved away from the door.

His gaze raked over her body from head to toe. She warmed under his scrutiny.

"You're beautiful," he said as he entered. "You take my breath away, Jordan."

Damn. Spoken in that husky tone of his, she moistened, her body opening and arousing instantaneously.

How did he do that to her?

Okay, so the compliment pleased her more than she cared to admit. She didn't want to ponder the whys of that either, mentally adding it to her previous list of questions best left unanswered.

"Thank you."

"You're welcome." Sam handed her the flowers. "Most women seem to like roses, but you don't seem the roses type to me."

The bouquet of lilies and freesia was beautiful and smelled intoxicating, like warm summer nights near the ocean, tropical and sensual.

"Thank you, Sam. They're lovely, and you're right. I'm not the roses type at all." How did he know that? Most men didn't. If they bothered to bring her flowers at all, they were typically roses. But the bouquet in her arms was by far the most beautiful she'd ever received.

"You ready to go?" He seemed impatient, and surprisingly, a bit nervous as he stood in the foyer.

"Sure. Let me put these in water before we leave."

As Jordan stood in the kitchen and filled a vase with water, she thought maybe she'd be able to endure the evening after all.

"Okay," she said as she returned and grabbed her purse from the hall stand near the door. "I'm ready."

They walked outside and headed down the porch steps. Jordan stopped dead in her tracks as she reached the driveway. Gone was Sam's beat-up old pickup truck, and in its place stood a sleek black Corvette. When she looked over at him, he shrugged and opened the door to her side of the car.

"I invested well in the market. It paid off."

Every time she thought she knew everything there was to know about Sam, he shocked her by revealing something new. The man was full of surprises.

* * * * *

Sam tried hard to concentrate on driving, but found it increasingly difficult with Jordan's long legs in view next to him. And her dress, oh God that dress.

When she'd opened the front door, his first thought was that she looked like sin. Wicked, hot, and damn flaming desirable. The flimsy silk did nothing to disguise her curves. Her breasts and hips were outlined perfectly as the dress draped across her body like a lover's caress. It was all Sam could do not to groan out loud in agony.

The jeans he wore left no room to mask a hard-on. And damn if one hadn't popped up, full-blown, in seconds. He couldn't help that his mind immediately went into sexual overdrive and imagined tossing that dress up and plunging inside her right there in the foyer.

And her scent, that unmistakable combination of perfume and woman, mingled together, intoxicating his senses, making clear and coherent thought almost impossible. Sam was certain he thrust the flowers at her like a schoolboy on his first date, and probably didn't mutter anything intelligible other than a caveman grunt.

Didn't she know what she was doing to him? How could someone who made it so clear she wasn't interested in him act and dress as if she were preparing a seduction unparalleled by Samson's Delilah herself?

Stealing a glance in Jordan's direction he was rewarded with the sight of her stretching to accommodate the low seats of the 'vette. The silk pulled across her breasts, accentuating her nipples which were poorly disguised under something that did little to meet the definition of a bra.

Adjusting himself in his seat to accommodate his growing discomfort, Sam tried to think of some idle conversation to get his mind off the sex goddess riding in the car next to him. Maybe math, or baseball.

Thankfully, she began to speak and his thoughts switched from turning off onto the next dirt road and ravaging her on the spot, to polite interest in her conversation.

"Where are we going?"

He tried to form a coherent sentence, but visions of silky legs and sweaty bodies put all other thoughts out of his mind.

Think, dumbass, think.

He needed to get his mind out of Jordan's pants and focus on her question. Pants? Now that thought brought even more erotic visions to the forefront, like whether or not Jordan wore panties.

"Huh?" was all he could manage as a response.

"Dinner? We are going to dinner aren't we?" She was looking at him like he had two heads.

Damn! Dinner.

Focus, man! You'd think you hadn't had sex with a woman in ages. Oh wait, you haven't had sex with a woman in ages!

"Oh yeah. Sorry, I was thinking about baseball. I thought we'd eat at Boudreaux."

More than baseball stats were going to be necessary to make it through dinner. He didn't know how he was going survive looking at her and inhaling her feminine scent without throwing her on top of the dinner table and having *her* for dinner instead. It was going to be a long night.

* * * * *

At the mention of Boudreaux, Jordan nodded in approval. A lovely restaurant on the outskirts of town, Boudreaux had been around since the early 1900s. They served a cornucopia of dishes, from down-home southern cooking to French cuisine. Remembering some of the delicious meals she had eaten there, she eagerly anticipated sampling their fare again after so long.

They pulled into the restaurant parking lot and headed inside. She wondered what had come over Sam, thinking maybe he didn't feel well. He seemed uncomfortable in the car, squirming and silent. Then when he finally started talking, he carried on an entire conversation about baseball!

Sitting in the car with Sam had been torture. His cologne wafted over her in waves every time he moved. Not only did she find the cologne he wore appealing, but his natural masculine scent evoked primitive desires that she was unable to squash. Like the desire to run her fingers through his hair, draw him close to her, and inhale deeply of his potent masculinity. Try as she might to find the experience unpleasant, she couldn't.

They were seated at a small intimate table for two in the corner of the restaurant. She wondered whose idea that was, or if the hostess just assumed they wanted privacy.

She took a moment to glance around. The place hadn't changed in a hundred years, and definitely not as long as she had been eating there. Boudreaux was actually a former plantation home, and its beauty and reminder of the genteel days before the war were still evident. The restaurant was filled with antique furnishings, brocade draperies and nineteenth-century art. The ambiance of the old south dominated the décor, making one feel as if transported back in time to long forgotten days.

Their waitress appeared and Sam suggested they share a bottle of wine. He surprised Jordan with his expert knowledge of vintage and brand. She complimented his choice.

"You think because I live here I only know beer brands?"

"I didn't say that, did I?"

"You didn't have to. I read the surprise on your face. Just because I live in a small town doesn't mean I'm a dumb hillbilly."

Now where did that come from? Give the man a compliment and he thinks he's been insulted. "Boy, you're touchy this evening. I wasn't ridiculing you; I was complimenting your taste in wine. Don't jump all over me because of something you're assuming I think."

"You're right. Sorry. Guess I must be a little oversensitive about how you perceive me."

Sam? Sensitive? Who was he kidding? Jordan had tried her best to insult him six ways from Sunday with no luck. The man had a hide thick as a boar.

He reached across the table and took her hand. "Let's start over, okay? I want this to be a special evening for us."

Uh-oh. A special evening. That phrase foreshadowed events Jordan didn't want to think about.

"Look," she said in as matter-of-fact a way as she could. "You and I both know you set up this so-called date this afternoon. It's not like a real date. We're not a couple, so don't get your hopes up. Nothing is going to happen tonight."

He gave her a wicked smile that sent her pulse racing. "We'll see, won't we?"

After ordering dinner, Jordan sipped her wine, a smooth Merlot, warm and full-bodied, but not too tart. It was very good and she had to admit Sam had made an excellent choice. Finally she began to relax.

"Tell me about your life," Sam asked as he leaned back in his chair and lazily traced his finger around the rim of his wineglass.

"What do you want to know?"

"How about what you've been doing since you left Magnolia? I know you've been involved in theater, but I'm interested in how you picked that career."

"It was a simple choice for me," she explained. "When I graduated high school, I was awarded a drama scholarship at NYU. My admissions counselor told me I had written a great essay."

"About what?"

Jordan remembered it well. She had poured her heart and soul into that essay, knowing it held the key to her future. "I wrote about dreams, and one of my dreams was to own a theater. I wanted to pursue a drama degree, then work in a city where I could put my love of theater to use."

He arched a brow and refilled her wineglass. "Go on."

Jordan wrapped her fingers around the glass, watching the red liquid swirl back and forth. "Not much more to tell. I went to college, took courses in theater and production, and was lucky to find a part-time job at one of the off-Broadway theaters. I made some good contacts and when I graduated was offered a position at the Manhattan Community Playhouse I started out doing grunt stuff and slowly worked my way up. I've been Assistant Director there for the past six years."

"Are you happy?"

Her gaze flew up to meet his. "Of course. I love my job."

A small smile lifted the corners of his mouth. "I wasn't referring to your job. I meant are you happy in your personal life?"

"What do you mean?"

"I mean, what do you do for fun? Do you date? Go out with friends? Surely you don't work twenty-four hours a day, Jordan. You must have a social life."

Red bells clanged in her head. This was getting too personal, and delving into forbidden territory. "Um, I'm usually busy with work. I don't have much time for a social life."

Ugh. That sounded pathetic even to her.

"What about sex?" He leaned toward her, his blue eyes compelling her to respond.

"What about it?" She looked down once again at the glass of wine. How did such a safe subject like her work get turned into a discussion about her sex life?

Or lack of one.

He laughed. "What about it? Do I have to be more specific? Do you date men? Do you have a sex life? It's not like you're sixteen years old. You must have a love life somewhere."

She was *not* going to discuss her sex life with Sam. Even if she had one she wouldn't discuss it with him.

"Well, if I do or I don't it's none of your business." Why couldn't they just talk about the weather or something? Maybe she could get him back on the subject of baseball.

"I see." His smile changed to a smirk.

"You see what?"

"It's obvious."

"What's obvious?"

"You must not like sex."

Really, she wanted to scream. Sam's leaps in logic were Olympian. Instead she settled for, "Excuse me?"

"It's perfectly clear to me. You ran from me when you were younger and I kissed you, and it seems you've been running your whole life."

Now her blood was boiling. "I'll have you know that I've had lots of sex, and hundreds of love affairs."

His eyes widened, then seconds later he burst out laughing so loud he drew stares from the other diners.

"Stop that," she admonished in a harsh whisper. "You're drawing attention. And what's so funny?"

"Sorry," he said, still chuckling. Taking one of her curls in his hand and threading it through his fingers, he whispered, "I don't buy it for a second. I don't know what your level of experience with men is, but I'll bet you a million dollars that you've had very little romance in your life, and if you've had *some* sex, it hasn't been great, and it hasn't happened in awhile."

Damn him for his intrusive questions. And damn him for being right on the money about her sex life. "Look. This subject is out of bounds. I don't want to discuss it further. Change the topic or I'm leaving."

A smug smile crossed his face as if he'd just won a battle. "Okay. You're the boss. Let's talk about something else."

Somehow she knew she'd been given only a temporary reprieve, and this subject would be revisited again before the night was through.

They discussed the house over dinner, a safe enough subject. Sam shared his plans for the rest of the repairs, and made some suggestions on improvements to the property. She was impressed with his ideas and knowledge. He seemed to know a lot about many different things.

"Tell me," she asked between mouthfuls of delicious grilled sea bass, "How did you get into the construction business?"

"It's a long story. You sure you want to hear it all?"

"Yes I do." The mystery of Sam's disappearance after the high school dance still played through her mind.

"I joined the Army when I was eighteen. I got into some trouble a couple months before graduation, a stupid mistake actually, but one that could have sent me in the wrong direction."

"What mistake?"

"I stole a car."

Okay, now he had her complete attention. "You did? When?"

"I was really pissed off at life back then. Typical teenage rebellion, no direction in my life, not knowing what I wanted to do, but not being satisfied with living here. I think I just wanted some attention. Maybe I needed a catalyst to force some decision about my destiny. I don't know. Anyway, one night I broke into a car, hot-wired the ignition and took it for a joyride to the next county. The highway patrol picked me up and brought me back here to jail."

Jordan was astounded. She had never heard this story before, didn't know he had gotten arrested.

"Anyway, the highway patrol officer who arrested me was a friend of my dad's. Needless to say, my dad was really pissed. He got me released and informed me my choices were to get my butt into the military or rot in jail. Not being completely stupid, I took the military option and joined the Army. I shipped out a couple weeks later."

"That's why I didn't see you after the Spring Fling dance."

He nodded. "Exactly. I stole the car that same weekend." Grinning at her, he said, "It must be your fault. You ran away from me and I was so distraught I immediately turned to a life of crime."

Jordan rolled her eyes. "Oh please. Don't be an idiot. What happened next?"

"Well it turns out I had an aptitude for military life. Once boot camp knocked that chip off my shoulder, I did quite well at infantry school. After I went through special training and jump school, I went into Special Forces."

"Which means what?" It was all she could do to keep the astonishment out of her voice. She'd had no idea of the life he led after high school.

His smile didn't reach his eyes. "Just means I was legally allowed to sneak in to foreign countries. Espionage. You know. Spy games. Was interesting work, for sure, but that kind of life wears on you after a while. I'd moved up fast and became an officer, but after the Gulf War I lost my taste for it. Finished up my duty and got out, deciding it was time I go to college."

She hadn't known about any of this. Of course, she wouldn't know anything about him, or anyone else in this town. Once she left, she rarely came back and when she did it was only for short visits with Grandma.

"What didn't you like about the military?"

Pushing his now empty plate to the side, he replied, "Being in the Gulf War was the final act for me. One of my best friends was killed there. Kind of puts a new perspective on your life when you watch someone you care about die right in front of your eyes. I decided then and there the kind of life I had been leading wasn't for me. I wanted to go home, get an education, put down some roots and make a stable life for myself. So I did."

Pain laced his voice. The horrors he must have gone through were unimaginable. She laid her hand over his. "I'm sorry about your friend. It must have been terrible for you."

He nodded. "It was. I won't lie about that. I'm not so tough that I didn't care about my friends. It was very hard seeing him die. It changed my life."

Jordan felt overwhelming pain for Sam. She couldn't imagine what he went through, wouldn't even try to guess how he felt. But she did know it hurt him; she could read the pain and sadness in his eyes. What a horrible experience, and one that would definitely change someone's life. No wonder he wanted the comforts of home after that.

They were both lost in their own thoughts as the waitress picked up their dinner plates and brought them coffee.

"Tell me about college."

"I came back here and went to the University of South Carolina, where I graduated with a degree in business. That's where I met Tony. During college Tony and I worked for my uncle's construction company part-time during the school year and full-time in the summers. We both liked working with our hands, enjoyed building things. One thing led to another and we formed *TNT Construction* after we got out of college, and set up shop here in Magnolia. And that's my life in a nutshell."

There was much more depth to Sam than she had originally thought. He had experiences she couldn't possibly understand, and had seen and done more than she ever would. Yet he was happiest here in Magnolia.

But he didn't mention his ex-wife. And Jordan really wanted to know what happened there.

Her thoughts were interrupted when Millie and Ed Grayson stopped by their table. Jordan wasn't surprised to see them. They must have been designated the official eavesdroppers over her date with Sam. With Millie around, a report would surely be filed with the entire town by morning.

"Well, well, well, just look at the two of you," Millie said enthusiastically. "All dressed up and out together. What a lovely couple you make. It's about time you got her to go out with you, Sam," she said with a wink.

Sam grinned like a kid as he stood and hugged Millie. "She kept telling me no, Millie. Thank God I had the backup team around today to give her a little push in my direction."

Jordan smiled tightly and made light conversation. She felt on display. Of course Sam was eating it all up, enjoying the attention and making a much bigger deal than necessary over their so-called date.

"Now you two go back to enjoying each other. And don't keep our director out too late tonight."

They said their goodbyes to Millie and Ed, and finished their coffee.

"Are you ready to go?" Sam asked as he paid the bill.

She couldn't wait to get away from all the prying eyes of Magnolia's Matchmaking, Incorporated.

And although she'd learned more about Sam tonight than she had ever known before, it still didn't change things. In a few weeks she'd be going back to New York, and he would be staying in Magnolia.

She didn't want the pull of attraction she felt whenever he was around. Nor did she care for the way her mind conveniently forgot her goals and dreams and focused instead on gorgeous blue eyes and a fine ass.

Priorities, Jordan. Fucking Sam isn't on the top ten list.

So, pleasant as the evening had been, she was relieved their date was over. She had done her part, had gone out to dinner with Sam, and now she could go home.

Chapter Seven

"This isn't the way home." Jordan cast a suspicious glare in Sam's direction.

He didn't even turn to look at her. "I know."

After they'd left the restaurant he took the opposite direction from Jordan's home. What was he up to now, and how much more of this ordeal could she take?

"Where are you taking me? I'd like to go home now, if you don't mind."

Glancing over at her, he smiled enigmatically. "I want to show you something. It won't take long. Promise."

She could either start an argument, or go see what he wanted her to see. Sighing, she decided she'd endure a few more minutes in the close confines of the car with Sam. A few more minutes of torture, while she stole glances at his incredible profile, his thick black hair, his piercing blue eyes, and inhaled the heady scent of his cologne. Definitely torture, but she was tough. She could take it for a bit longer.

Too preoccupied looking at Sam to notice where they were headed, she was shocked when he pulled into Maggie's Bluff, so named because the area sat on top of a bluff overlooking Magnolia.

Good lord, this was where all the high school kids used to go to make out. She had never personally experienced the place, but she knew where it was, and had heard enough about it from the other kids at school.

"You're kidding, right?"

Sam parked the car and turned to look at her. "Just thought we'd digest a bit and look at the stars. It's a nice night, and I wasn't quite ready to take you home. You don't mind, do you?"

"Mind? Of course not. Why would I mind?" Right. And why were her palms sweaty? How old was she anyway? Perhaps age was irrelevant at the town make-out point.

"Let's get out and look at those stars." He exited the car and walked around to Jordan's door, opening it and offering his hand.

Reluctantly, Jordan placed her sweaty hand in Sam's and allowed him to pull her out of the car. But instead of releasing her hand, he continued to hold it as they walked side by side to the edge of the bluff. Jordan could feel his warmth and strength as he held her small hand firmly in his large one. Well *his* palms certainly weren't sweaty.

They reached the edge of the bluff and Sam moved Jordan in front of him. "Beautiful," he murmured against her ear.

Jordan had to agree. The night was perfectly clear and thousands of stars were visible in the summer sky, so close she had to resist the urge to reach out and touch them. A slight breeze blew away the humid discomfort of the day, and the lights of Magnolia below mirrored the celestial ones above, appearing like twin images.

"Yes, it is," she replied, marveling at a sight she never got to experience amongst the towering buildings of New York City. "I've never seen anything quite like it before."

"I meant you, not the view." Sam whispered huskily in her ear as he wrapped his arms around her. Close enough to feel his breath ruffle her hair. Close enough to feel his chest pressing against her back, his arms wound around her middle, just under her breasts.

Her nipples hardened and she was afraid to take another breath.

"Surely you've seen this sight before. The view up here has always been like this."

"I've never been up here before." She was mesmerized by the incredible beauty of the lights flickering above and below her and the exquisite sensation of being held in Sam's arms. There was a sense of peace and tranquility up here. Not a sound other than the trees lightly rustling in the soft summer breeze. It was like being completely alone in the universe. Alone with Sam.

He turned her to face him. "What do you mean you've never seen it before?" The soft moonlight shined over his inquisitive face.

"I told you. I've never been here before tonight." Great. Another thing to be embarrassed about. Who'd wanted to date the drama nerd in high school anyway?

"Damn, Jordan, that surprises the hell out of me. All the years you lived here, all through high school, no boy ever brought you up here?"

She laughed at the surprise in his voice. "No, Sam, no one ever brought me up here before. I guess I've missed out on an incredible sight all these years. I had no idea it was so lovely."

"That's not all you missed out on, sugar." As if a cloud passed over, his eyes suddenly darkened. A spark of deviltry twinkled in the turquoise orbs. "You know why the high school kids come up here, don't you?"

"I'm not completely naïve, Sam. Of course I know what goes on up here. I just never…"

"Never got to experience it yourself?"

She nodded, feeling stupidly inept, vestiges of the timid girl she was in high school returning to haunt her. Jordan never thought she was missing anything before by not coming here. Sure, she'd heard all the stories about who hooked up with whom on Maggie's Bluff, who got pregnant in who's Chevy. Typical small-town gossip. But not once had she ever longed to have a guy bring her up here.

Why did she feel that longing now? With Sam? And why did it irk her that he obviously had fond memories of this place? Of course he had brought other girls to Maggie's Bluff. Sam was popular in high school, the bad boy every good girl wanted to date. It shouldn't bother her all these years later, so why did it?

"I think it's time someone showed you what you missed." His voice lowered to barely above a whisper. He caressed her bare shoulders, sweeping away her hair and capturing one of the curls before it fell behind her back, letting it slide through his fingers as his gaze burned into her.

"No."

"Still scared?" He was baiting her.

She tried to pull away from his grasp but he wouldn't let her go. "I'm not scared of anything, Sam Tanner, and especially not you. I'm no longer sixteen years old. I know exactly what I'm doing and what I want. And this isn't it."

"I think you're lying. You and I have been playing a game these past few days, Jordan. A game of cat and mouse. I'm ready to pounce. You ready to be eaten?"

Oh, God. Oh, dear God. She didn't want those images in her mind. Primal images, of lying spread-eagled on the ground while Sam ate her pussy until she screamed into the quiet night.

"No." Her heart pounded, perspiration pooled between her breasts, and her panties grew wet from her arousal.

"Prove it." A glint of humor and challenge sparkled in his eyes. "Kiss me once—one hard, hot kiss. Then tell me you don't feel anything, and I'll let it go."

If she kissed him, she'd never let go. A hunger gnawed at her. She was starving for this—for sex, for once in her life desperate to be wild and free.

She'd never survive it. "I don't have to prove anything."

"Coward."

"I am *not* a coward. I just refuse to play this childish game with you."

"That's because you're afraid of me. One kiss, Jordan. Just one hard, hot kiss. Give me all you've got and that'll be the end of it."

Okay, one kiss. She could do this. All she had to do was give him one little kiss, and then she'd be free of him. A quick peck to get Sam off her back forever. Well worth it to save her sanity.

"You're on." Leaning into him and grabbing his head between her hands, she smashed her lips into his, grinding her mouth against his. As fast as she could, she ended it, stepping back with a satisfied smile on her face. There, she had done it. She had kissed him, felt nothing, and now it was over.

Except Sam was laughing.

All right. The kiss hadn't been *that* bad, had it?

Moving forward into the space she had just created, he leaned toward her until their noses were practically touching. His breath brushed her cheek as their eyes met.

"Baby, that was definitely a hard kiss, but hardly a hot one. The deal was one hard, *hot* kiss." Sliding one hand behind her neck and the other around her waist, he pulled her to him, his muscled body pressed intimately against hers. "Since you're unwilling to do it the right way, I will."

His lips descended over hers and turned her world upside down.

Jordan had been kissed by men before. But not like this. Never like this. Not with this kind of passion and intimacy. Sam gave her what she'd been unwilling to give him, what she'd been afraid to give him. A kiss with feeling behind it, with emotion.

A kiss that spoke of desire and need, of secrets in the dark. Secrets she was desperate to uncover.

He explored the textures of her mouth with his tongue, sliding his lips back and forth over hers as their tongues played in a sensual rhythm. Jordan's trembling body clung to his for support as his strong arms held her in his embrace.

There wasn't a part of her body that didn't scream out for his touch. As his hands roamed over her, she couldn't stifle the moans that escaped her lips, encouraging his exploration of her throat, her arms, her back. Everywhere he touched ignited flames along her nerve endings until she could barely stand. If he hadn't been holding her in his arms she'd have surely fallen to the ground.

But she wanted to touch him, too. For too many years she'd wondered what would have happened if she'd taken that step with him, if she'd allowed herself to realize her feelings.

Just one damn time she didn't want to be afraid.

She slid her hands over his arms. His biceps tensed as she grasped them in an attempt to pull herself closer to him. Tearing her mouth from his, she trailed kisses down his chin and throat, feeling his pulse beat erratically in his neck as she touched that point where his blood pounded in a frantic rhythm.

Knowing Sam was as affected by their kissing as she was excited her beyond belief. She nipped his shoulder lightly with her teeth. He groaned and slid his hands through her hair, pulling her closer, wrapping the strands around his fists and dragging her lips once again over his own.

Her knees weakened. She was leaning over Sam's arm, practically prone. Then suddenly he lifted her into his arms, never once breaking the contact of his mouth on hers. He walked over to a nearby picnic table and laid her down.

Jordan opened her eyes to see his luminous eyes poring over her. The full moon clearly illuminated every feature of his face and body. His eyes raked boldly over her, searching her own for a response. She couldn't tear her eyes away from him as he held her pinned with the dark passion of his heavy-lidded gaze.

Tentatively he ran a hand along her bare arm, lightly trailing his fingertips from her shoulder to her wrist. He twined his fingers with hers and pulled her hand to his mouth, pressing light kisses against her knuckles.

"This game has gone on way too long. It's time to end it. I want you, Jordan, and unless you get up from this table right now and walk away, I intend to have you."

Her breath caught on a gasp at the passionate promise in his husky voice. The way his gaze fixed on her in such an intimate way should have caused her to turn away, but she didn't. They were locked together and she was helpless to break the bond. Waves of passion and need coursed through her blood until she wanted to cry out in frustration.

Say it. Say the words. Nothing bad will happen. You're not your mother, Jordan.

"I want you, Sam. Now."

The cool metal of the table pressed against her bare legs as he leaned over her. He placed his hands on either side of her hips to brace himself against the table, then dipped his head and met her eager mouth again. In the process of kissing her senseless, he slid his hands along her hips to the place where her skimpy dress met her thighs. Sliding the dress up with his hands, he leaned against her, pressing his erection against her sex.

The contact was electric. His cock was blazing hot, searing her weeping cunt. Jordan moaned and felt more moisture seep from her.

"God, Jordan," Sam groaned between clenched teeth. He moved his body against hers, slowly. "I want you. I've wanted you for so long." Then he took her mouth again, his slow, sensual assault on her lips eliciting moans of pleasure.

His hands roamed everywhere, sliding along every exposed area of her skin, evoking shivers throughout her nerve endings. An aching need pulsed between her legs, her thin silk panties moistening with her desire. He continued to kiss her deeply as he ran his hands over her belly, sliding his pinkie into the ring attached to her navel.

"This is fucking sexy as hell," he said, leaning over to lick around the jeweled ring attached to her belly. "I would never have thought you'd have a piercing."

It had been a whim, something silly on a boring weekend. A couple colleagues had wanted to stop in the piercing parlor, and not wanting to be the stick-in-the-mud, she'd gone in with them.

At that moment, she'd wanted to be daring. She didn't want to be afraid, and hell, she had no one in her life to tell her what to do, so she'd gone ahead and had her navel pierced. It made her feel decadent, a little wild, all those things that weren't really her.

"I never knew you were a wild child," he said, leaning up and pressing his erection against her throbbing sex.

"I'm not." She wasn't. He didn't know her at all.

"Oh, I think that wild creature lurks within you, Jordan. You just don't let her out very often."

She didn't know what he was talking about. She wasn't wild at all. She never took chances. She never—

Look at her. She wasn't wild? Yeah, right. She was spread-eagled on a picnic table in a public place, writhing underneath a hot, sexy man with a hard-on. This was as wild as she'd ever been.

She should be appalled at her behavior, but dammit, she was tired of always being safe. She wanted Sam touching her, kissing her. She wanted his cock in her pussy and his mouth on her clit.

Now would be good. She lifted her hips, hoping he'd fuck her, lick her, anything to assuage the incessant throbbing ache inside her.

But instead he stood and moved his hands toward her breasts, resting his palms just underneath them. Her nipples hardened and she moved without thinking, begging him without speaking to touch her.

"You want me to touch you?"

"Yes. Dammit, yes! Please, Sam."

She heard her own voice but didn't recognize it. Husky, aroused and demanding, it was like a part of her she'd never seen before had just surfaced. The part that was wild and wanton, the part she'd hidden for so long. The part Sam said lurked inside her.

Maybe she didn't know herself as well as she thought.

When his palms grazed lightly over her breasts, she instinctively arched her back, filling his hands. He rubbed his fingertips against her nipples, and electric jolts of desire arced from her breasts to that throbbing spot between her legs.

Her response to Sam shocked her. There was so much more to what they were doing, to what she was feeling, than she had ever experienced before. She wasn't inexperienced. But with other men it had been different. Just sex. Sex without intimacy was easy, required nothing but a physical response and no emotional attachment. But like it or not, her bond with Sam had always been emotional.

And now, as her lips sought his, hungrily responding to every stroke of his tongue, Jordan realized the difference. What they were doing implied much more than just two people who craved an intimacy driven by physical lust. This involved the heart. Caring, wanting, desiring something beyond the physical.

She tensed as the old fears came back to haunt her. Like a cold wind, she chilled, reaching for Sam's hands and pushing him away.

"I can't do this."

He stilled for a moment and made eye contact with her. "Why not?"

"Because."

"Because I make you feel something?" He demonstrated by skimming her rib cage, with each movement of his hand raising her dress higher and higher until it rode her hips, baring her wet panties to his probing gaze.

"No. I don't—"

"Don't tell me you don't feel, Jordan." He swept one hand down over her belly and lower, slipping his fingers inside the tiny scrap of silk, gently caressing her erect clit.

She gasped, sucked in a breath as if she hadn't had oxygen in too long, and whimpered her need for him.

The hell with fear. She wanted this!

"You have needs, baby. Needs I can take care of for you. I think it's been too long for you, Jordan, and you need to come."

"Yes," she said, finally giving up her internal war. "Make me come, Sam."

He reached for the strings at her hips, untying them and pulling the fabric away from her hot, wet flesh.

The throbbing reached painful levels, making her want to reach between her legs and massage the sensation until she came. She lifted her head and saw Sam staring between her legs.

"Such a pretty little pussy, baby. You know I can smell you when you're aroused and near me?"

No, she didn't know that, but she understood it. His scent was so familiar to her that whenever he was near all she wanted to do was breathe.

"Your scent is so sweet, like summer musk and wildflowers. God, you make me hard. I can barely stand to be near you sometimes. It makes my cock strain and all I want to do is strip you down and bury myself inside you."

She'd never been wanted like that before. Such a heady, powerful feeling, to know that she could make Sam need like that.

"I'm here now. Take me."

He tore his gaze away from her pussy and looked at her, his lips curling in a feral, dangerous smile. "Oh I'm going to take it. Any way I want to. You ready for that, sugar?"

"Yes." More than ready.

"But first I have to taste that sweet cream, see if you taste as good as you smell." He dropped to his knees and spread her legs, drawing closer and closer to her quivering pussy. When his tongue snaked out and lapped up her cream, she arched her hips off the table, moaning loud and long.

This is what it felt like to be pleasured by someone she cared about. No, not cared about—desired. She couldn't bring emotion into play here. Too dangerous. But oh, how he made her feel! Like climbing onto a cloud and floating, while thousands of hands touched her, took her to a higher plane of pleasure.

Fear melted away and desire took over, her mind focused on his touch, his hot mouth and the delicious things he did to her.

He lapped at her then, short, quick strokes that drove her to the edge and back so many times she was near tears. He seemed to have an inherent ability to know which stroke would send her catapulting into oblivion, and stopping one lick short of that.

"Sam, please," she begged, not caring anymore, knowing only that she needed what he could give her.

He moved away, his hot breath pulsing across her swollen sex. "You taste like the sweetest dessert in the south, Jordan. I could eat you all night."

But he wouldn't have all night, because the next long swipe of his tongue against her clit and her hips rocketed off the table as her orgasm washed over her. She soaked his tongue with her juices as her climax pulsed on and on for what seemed like an eternity.

Through it, Sam continued to lave at her flesh, drinking in her climax and covering her clit with his lips. He finally moved away, stood up and just watched her.

She could barely lift her head, but what she saw shocked her. Never had she seen a man's face so fierce with desire, his intentions so clear in the harsh frown, the clenched jaw, the little tic that pulsed at his temple.

His cock strained against his jeans, long, hard, thick, and she desperately wanted to reach out and touch him.

Hell, she wanted to devour him in one gulp, take him to the same place he'd taken her, and then start all over again.

She never wanted to leave Maggie's Bluff, finally realizing that she hadn't missed anything in her youth but fumbling and excuses. What she was missing was what she had right now. With Sam.

And she never wanted to let him go.

With that need to possess him, to become one with him, fear began to creep into the haze of desire.

This couldn't happen. Her growing feelings for Sam made her vulnerable and weak. Like her mother. And like her mother, she could be susceptible to making the wrong choices. Sam Tanner was the wrong choice; she already knew that.

And like her mother, she'd let her desires influence her into making a disastrous decision. One she'd have to rectify right now.

"No!" she said forcefully as she leaned up and scurried away. "I can't do this."

Sam stilled for a moment. He was breathing heavily, erratic gasps of air. He leaned his hands onto the table, his fingers just inches from her thighs. "What's wrong, Jordan?"

"I just can't do this," she said, trying to calm her own erratic pulse.

"We already did."

"No, we didn't. You did, I mean I did, but we...oh hell!" She wasn't even making any sense. Slipping off the table, she reached for her panties and crushed them in her fist, not even bothering to slip them back on. She pulled her dress down over her thighs and turned away from Sam.

"Did I do something wrong?" he asked quietly.

She shook her head. "No, you did nothing wrong, Sam. I just can't."

"Can't what?"

"Can't do this," she repeated, mortified she had let it get this far without stopping him. She may be a coward, but she was not a tease. "With you. I'm sorry, but it's wrong. We're wrong."

"I don't understand. What we just shared was hot for both of us. I felt your response. Hell, Jordan, I've never seen someone come with such abandon before. So what's really the issue here?"

Heat flamed her face. Yeah, she'd been abandoned all right. Abandoned of all her common sense.

How was she going to explain to him that she wanted him too much to have him? That she didn't want to end up like her mother, chasing after a man who had his pick of women, and would most likely end up sampling all of them? How could she tell him she didn't trust him, and she didn't trust herself to be near him?

She didn't want to hurt him, but the best way out of this would be to make him angry with her. A coward's way out, she knew, but then she didn't feel very strong at the moment. If Sam tried any harder to convince her she had feelings for him, she'd be ripping his clothes off right here and now.

She had acting experience. Might as well give it her best performance. Turning to him, she gave him her coolest expression. "Well, yes, it was mildly entertaining, but I've had better."

"You've—had—better." He repeated her words slowly as if he hadn't quite heard her correctly.

"Yes. And while the orgasm was good, I've changed my mind about going any further. After I thought about it, I realized I have too many other things going on in my professional life to get involved with anyone on a personal level." Stealing a glance in his direction, she watched his expression darken, that tic against his temple pulsing stronger now.

Well, he was definitely getting angry. She'd better finish him off now, while she still had the courage.

Turning to face him, she laid her hand condescendingly on his forearm. "The orgasm was fine, Sam, and I thank you for the diversion. And for dinner. Can we go home now? I really have a lot to do before tomorrow and it's getting late." With a quick turn on her heel, she hurried toward the car, got into the passenger seat and waited.

He stood there for a minute, watching her from his spot on the bluff. Jordan wished she could see the expression on his face, but was glad she couldn't. It hurt her to say those things to him after the intimacy they'd just shared, but she had no choice.

Finally he stomped down the hill to the car. Taking a deep breath, she hoped her lies had worked and he was angry enough not to speak to her on the drive home. No such luck as he got in and slammed the door, turned in his seat and grabbed her chin, forcing her to look into his angry eyes.

"You may think you're a good actress, Miss New York Drama Director," he said, his jaw clenched as he ground out the words. "But I know you better than you know yourself. You were hot tonight. For me. For sex. For what could happen between us that goes beyond that. You wanted it as much as I did, so don't give me that 'it didn't mean anything' line of bullshit." He released her chin and turned away from her.

He started the engine and peeled out of the gravel road onto the highway. He didn't speak to her until he pulled up in front of her house. When she moved to open the door, he reached for her wrist, forcing her to look in his direction.

"You're lying, Jordan. To me, and to yourself."

Miserably, she admitted to herself that he was right.

Chapter Eight

Sam was still seething when he arrived at Jordan's house the next morning. He sat in his truck in her driveway, still trying to figure out what the hell had gone wrong the night before.

They'd had a great dinner, good conversation, and she seemed to really enjoy his company. Jordan was fascinating to him, and not just in a physical way. They both started in the same place, but somehow ended up moving in opposite directions. That intrigued him. Sam wanted to know more about her, what drove her to leave Magnolia, and why she was afraid to come back. Mostly he wanted to know what scared her.

They had chemistry—damn combustible chemistry. Picturing the events of the night before, her legs spread on the picnic table, her pussy glistening with the juices of her arousal, had his cock twitching to life again. Once he'd gotten past her barriers, she was fire and passion and wanted him as much as he wanted her. And not just in a physical way, which surprised even Sam.

He'd wanted an emotional response from Jordan, wanted to know if what he felt was merely one-sided. And he'd gotten one. No one who kissed him with the kind of intensity Jordan did could be interested in him purely for sex.

Listen to him. He sounded more like a woman than a man. Gee, would Jordan still respect him in the morning?

He laughed, disgusted with himself for caring one way or the other what the hell she thought or felt.

Clearly she didn't care. She'd let him get her off, and then she was done. But he knew there was a lot more going on in her head. Jordan wasn't a selfish bitch. God knows he knew that personality type all too well—he'd married one.

No, something scared her last night. But what was it?

He raked his fingers through his hair, wondering why the fuck he was even thinking about it. She wasn't even his type. And he wasn't interested in her for a permanent relationship. She was a woman who craved what a large city could give her and would never be satisfied with a man who was content with his life in Magnolia.

Penny hadn't wanted him, either. At first she said she did, but then her true nature revealed itself and it was all about what his money could buy her, and where his success could take them.

And just like Penny, Jordan was all about money and success. Selling Belle Coeur and using the money to buy her own New York theater was a prime example of the type of woman Sam wanted nothing to do with. So what was it about her that kept him coming back, kept him interested?

Sex.

He kept reminding himself that all he really craved from Jordan was sex. Nothing else. And that's why he was so tied up in knots this morning. Yeah, she'd gotten off all right, and then left him hard and still hungering for a taste of her.

At that moment the woman he craved came flying out the front door, arms laden with papers. She wore a skirt and a blue T-shirt, and sandals with heels that looked like she'd break her neck if she turned too quickly.

When she spotted him, she hesitated at the top step, chewing her bottom lip as if trying to decide whether to walk toward him or run like hell in the opposite direction and lock herself in the house.

He gave her points for bravery as she slowly maneuvered the porch steps, coming to a stop in front of his truck window.

"Morning," she said in an almost-whisper, barely making eye contact with him as a slight blush stained her cheeks. Was she remembering last night too? She had been lying when she said she didn't feel anything. It was written all over her face.

He'd just have to prove to her that she did want him as much as he wanted her. He smiled as a plan began to formulate in his mind.

"Morning to you, too," he said cheerfully. He decided at that moment to let his anger about last night go. The only way she would open up would be if he got her to trust him. Making her angry wouldn't accomplish that goal. He glanced at her armful of papers. "Where are you headed in such a hurry today?"

"I...I have a meeting with the cast and I'm running late." He wagered she expected him to be angry about last night. Granted, she was a pretty good actress, but she wasn't *that* good. You couldn't fake the kind of passion she'd exhibited. And afterward, she'd wanted more.

She hesitated, as if she wanted to stay and talk. Maybe she felt bad about how things ended between them last night and wanted to make it up to him. Part of his new plan would be to make her wait. Make her pursue him for a change.

"I've got a lot to do around here," he said and began to open the truck door. She quickly stepped back. "Have fun today." Ignoring her, he reached into the back of the truck to gather his tools.

Looking out the corner of his eye, he suppressed a grin. She hadn't left yet, in fact, hadn't moved at all. She was probably waiting for him to make a remark, or flirt with her, or even yell at her. Not today. If Jordan Weston wanted him, she'd have to be the one to make the first move. Sam was going to try patience, at least for a while.

"Okay," she said hesitantly. "If you need anything, you know where I'll be."

"No problem. Same goes for you. If you need anything, you know where to find me."

He refused to even look at her, but hoped like hell she needed something from him, and that eventually she'd ask for it.

* * * * *

Rehearsals went well and the play was coming together nicely. The cast were all off-book now and knew their lines without prompting. Jordan was pleased with their musical talents. If she didn't know better, she could swear she was directing a professional group of actors. Admittedly, she was quite impressed.

She sat at her makeshift desk in the front room of the theater, making notes and waving to the cast members as they gathered their things and left.

Millie stopped at her desk. "So, sweetie, how did it go?"

"Rehearsals went great." Jordan looked up and smiled, remembering the duet Millie and Katie sang today. They had the most beautiful soprano voices she had ever heard, their melodies and harmonies blending in perfect sync. Of course Katie had always been a great singer. Jordan remembered listening to her in concerts in high school, and had even directed Katie in the senior play. Such a talent. Actually there were many talented people in Magnolia, more than she ever realized.

Laughing, Millie said, "I wasn't talking about rehearsals, I was talking about your date with Sam last night."

Katie chimed in as she walked up and stood next to her mother. "Oh yeah. Tell us all about it, Jordan. How was the date?"

She knew it had been too good to be true. Having spent the past couple hours in rehearsal without a single word about her date with Sam, she hoped that maybe they'd let it slide.

Wrong.

"It was fine."

"Fine. Fine? That's it, that's all you're going to say about it? Fine?" Millie obviously wanted more details. After all, how much gossip could she generate on a simple "fine"?

"We had a nice time. Great dinner, nice conversation, then he took me home." By way of Maggie's Bluff, but she wasn't about to mention that. She barely wanted to think about it herself. Could hardly think about it without blushing, remembering their heated kisses; the way Sam touched her, the way he...

No, she was *not* going there right now. Recalling the feel of his mouth and hands on her sent her mind wandering in directions she refused to follow.

Katie and Millie exchanged glances. They weren't buying it. Damn, she never could lie well.

"I saw the way Sam looked at you last night, and the way you looked back at him. There's something between the two of you."

"Maybe she doesn't want to talk about it, Mom."

Leave it to Katie to know when something was bothering her. Despite not keeping in touch as much over the years, they'd fallen into the old "best friends" routine so easily now that she was back. Jordan hadn't realized how much she missed having a good friend to confide in.

"I don't know. I really don't know what to do."

Katie gave her mother a look and a nod of her head.

"Well, sweetie," Millie said as she gathered her things. "I know you need someone your own age to talk to. Why don't you have a nice talk with Katie? But if you need me, I'll always be here for you." Millie kissed her on the cheek and left.

Jordan turned to Katie, but didn't know where to begin. She normally didn't entrust her feelings to anyone, never shared what was going on inside her. The less people knew about her the better. They already knew enough.

Thankfully, Katie took the lead. "Look. I know we haven't seen each other in awhile, but we're still friends. I've never stopped caring about you. You can talk to me, you know. I swear I won't repeat anything you say. Not even to my mom."

At Jordan's raised eyebrows, Katie laughed. "I know Mom's a busybody. Can't even keep her out of *my* business, let alone anyone else's."

Jordan grinned. "Your mom's great. She just likes to talk a lot."

"Right. About herself, about me, about everybody else in town. No use making excuses for her. I know she's a gossip. But I love her anyway."

How wonderful it must feel to have that kind of a bond with your mother. It was something Jordan didn't understand, but always felt envious of her friends who were close with their families.

"Seriously. You look like you could use a friend, and I'm here for you. Tell me what's bothering you."

Katie was right. She needed someone to talk to, someone to help her sort through her feelings for Sam. It was apparent she was making a mess of things for both of them.

"I don't know where to start." She put her papers to the side of the table and leaned back in the chair.

"Start with Sam. It's obvious he has feelings for you, and you have some for him too, don't you?"

She paused before answering, surprised when the first words out of her mouth were "Yes, I do. But I don't want to."

"Why not?"

"Because, it'll never work between us."

"Again, why not?"

"It's complicated."

Katie smiled patiently. "I've got time. Explain it to me."

Jordan had never trusted anyone enough to talk to them about her mother. But it was high time she did. Time to get it out in the open, instead of always holding it inside. Besides, Katie knew as much about her mother as anyone, at least as far as how Jordan felt about her.

"It's about my mother."

Katie nodded. "Go on."

"You know what she was like, how many men she dated, how often she'd skip town for days at a time with no word to anyone."

"I know it was hard on you."

"Understatement. I always hated those guys. She had a knack for choosing the wrong men. The charmers, the really good-looking men who only wanted one thing, and once they got it, dropped her like hot lava."

"Some women aren't cut out to be mothers, Jordan. Doesn't mean you'll follow the same path as she did."

"She ran, Katie. Not only did she ignore me most of my life, but she ran away from home and never came back. And she ran after a man." Not that it mattered anymore. Susie Lake Weston had ceased being Jordan's mother a long time ago.

"It's ancient history, Jordan. I know it still hurts...always will. But you can't let it dictate your life. Tell me how this affects you and Sam."

"I've never been seriously involved in a relationship, Katie. The men I've been with haven't attracted me in the least. They were..."

"Safe?"

Jordan smiled. "Yeah. Safe. They couldn't hurt me unless I cared about them. So I purposely dated men I had no emotional attachment to."

"Because of your mother."

"Right. I didn't want to be like her, and I'm afraid I will be. I can tell with Sam. He makes me crazy, Katie. I can't eat, I can't sleep, all I can think about is him. I want him so badly it hurts. And frankly, that scares the living hell out of me."

Katie took her hands and squeezed them. "You're not your mother. Nothing like her, in fact. I know what she did, everyone in town does. She was just a lost soul searching for some ideal that didn't exist. I've seen it happen before. And Sam is most definitely not like any of those guys your mom ran after. She chased losers. He's anything but a loser."

Jordan stood and walked over to the window, watching the late afternoon sun drift lazily over the town's Main Street. She crossed her arms and leaned against the window frame. Then she turned to Katie, unable to keep the pain from her voice.

"Logically, I know that. But in my heart I can't help but feel the same thing will happen to me that happened to my mother. Not one single man committed to her in the way she wanted. None of them loved her like she wanted to be loved. I think she set up unattainable expectations. I'd rather not get involved at all than risk becoming like her. I don't want to have those needs, those desires. If I don't have them, they can't hurt me."

Katie rose and walked over to Jordan, her sympathetic smile comforting.

"Don't you know that anyone worth loving is worth risking your heart for? Let me tell you something. I've known Sam Tanner my whole life. I've seen both his good side as well as his bad. And I saw what being married to Penny did to him. She was worthless, and couldn't appreciate a man like Sam if her life depended on it."

"Why didn't their marriage work?"

"It wasn't for lack of trying on Sam's part. He stuck with her as long as he could, much longer than any of us thought he should. And he was faithful as the day is long, Jordan. This is a small town, believe me if he wasn't we'd all know about it."

Jordan couldn't help but smile. She knew all about small-town grapevines. Once one person found out about something, everybody in town knew in less than twenty-four hours.

"He didn't want to hurt her, even though she was hurting him. A man like Sam makes a commitment and sticks with it. He's nothing like the men your mother ran after. Give him a chance."

Again, Sam surprised her. She couldn't picture him as a devoted husband, and definitely couldn't see him putting up with the kind of woman his ex-wife was. But that didn't mean he was right for her. And what difference did it make anyway? She wasn't staying in Magnolia. At best a relationship with Sam would be nothing more than a summer fling.

"I don't know if I can." She looked down at the floor, ashamed to admit her cowardice to Katie.

Katie took her by the shoulders, forcing her look up. "Look, spend some time with him. Get to know him instead of judging him by who you *think* he is. He comes off like a big sexist bully sometimes, but that's simply his way of hiding his pain. He's a true gentleman if you get past his bravado, Jordan. And if nothing else, just get out and have some fun while you're here. There's no harm in doing that, and no commitment is required."

In her heart she knew Katie was right. Sam was nothing like the men her mother chased. But they also had two completely different lifestyles. She didn't want to change hers, and Sam was happy where he was.

Still, what was the harm in spending a little time with Sam while she was here? Once they stopped biting each other's heads off, they actually enjoyed each other's company. And they definitely had chemistry. Explosive chemistry. If she could just concentrate on the physical, she might actually have some fun.

Finally she relaxed her shoulders, the tension easing. "I'll think about what you said."

Katie gathered her things, and Jordan opened the front door for her.

"Thanks, Katie," Jordan said as she leaned against the door. "I haven't had a friend in a long time. I've missed you."

Katie reached out and hugged her. "I've missed you too. And as far as Sam, maybe I just see something that you can't see." Laying her hand on Jordan's arm, she added, "Open your eyes, honey. What you need is right in front of you."

* * * * *

Sam's truck was right in front as Jordan pulled up to the house. He was loading it up with his tools, apparently finished with his work for the day.

She thought about everything Katie said during the drive home from the theater, and decided her friend was at least partially right. She may not want to have a permanent relationship with Sam, but she could certainly no longer deny her attraction to him. What was wrong with having a little fun?

People had sex without commitment all the time. She'd certainly done it before, and commitment had been the farthest thing from her mind. This was her chance to have mind-blowing sex with a man who truly rang all her bells. Why not experience some heated passion while she was here?

Now was as good a time to start as any. Besides, she still felt guilty about the way she'd treated him the day before, and figured it was time she made it up to him.

"Finished for the day?" She put on her brightest smile as she walked from her car towards his truck.

"Yeah." Turning to watch her approach, he asked, "How did it go today?"

"Great." Okay, so far so good. He didn't seem angry with her any longer. Maybe they could have dinner together tonight, or go to a movie. That would be fairly safe and harmless, and she was anxious to show him she was no longer afraid. She'd even be the one to ask him out this time. Wouldn't he be surprised at that?

One step at a time. Dinner, maybe a movie, and then they'd see where it went after that. She took a deep breath and said, "I was wondering if you were busy to —"

"Well, I'm beat," Sam interrupted and proceeded to yawn long and loud. "Think I'll head home and crash. See you tomorrow." He climbed into the truck and shut the door, then waved at her as he drove off.

Jordan closed her gaping mouth. Damn. Here she was, all prepared to boldly invite Sam out on a date, and he barely said ten words to her before he left. Well he sure picked a fine time to decide to ignore her!

That figured. When she wanted him to go away he was practically breathing down her neck at every turn. And now that she wanted him around, he became scarce. No wonder she didn't date much. She didn't understand the male mind at all.

She turned and started up the stairs, pausing to look up at the old house. And suddenly felt very lonely as she contemplated the long evening ahead.

* * * * *

It had gone even better than he'd planned.

Sam knew Jordan had wanted him to stay and talk when she came home yesterday, but that wasn't part of his plan. A bit of absence would make her heart grow fonder for him, and he got out of there as fast as he could.

Before he did something stupid, like ask her out tonight. Before he did what he really wanted to do when he first saw her get out of her car, those long tanned legs peeking out the driver's door, and the sensuous way she walked that she wasn't even aware of.

Yeah, he might have done something really idiotic then. Like take her in his arms, kiss her with all the wild abandon he felt whenever she was near, and carry her upstairs to her bed.

Then maybe something *really* dumb. Like remove her clothes bit by agonizing bit until she was naked. Then another dumb thing might have happened. He could have kissed every inch of her softly scented skin, ravishing her from head to toe with his tongue until she begged him to take her. Oh and then the final moronic act would be to sink his throbbing cock into her moist heat until she was wrapped hot and tight around him and make wild wicked love with her all night long.

Yeah, that sure would have been dumb. He groaned at the tightness in his shorts.

Idiot.

But if he was suffering sexual fantasies about the two of them, maybe Jordan was, too. Let her think about him for a while, make her want him a bit. Then let *her* make the first move.

He hoped he was patient enough to wait, and that Jordan wasn't patient at all. He was lonely and he wanted her. In his arms and in his bed. And if his guess was right, Jordan wanted him, too. But the next step was up to her.

Chapter Nine

There was nothing like summer rain in Magnolia. Jordan sipped her coffee at the kitchen table and looked out the window, watching it come down hard, pouring streams of water from the rooftop. Maybe it would cool things off and squelch some of the unbearable humidity of the past few days.

She rose and walked out the door onto the back porch. The smell of rain was intoxicating, bringing with it the sweet scent of the wisteria that clung tightly to the side of the house near the porch. Ancient gnarled branches covered with fragrant purple flowers bent and swayed in the onslaught of the rainstorm, but refused to give up their hold on the worn-out trellis.

Spying the cushioned wicker chairs on the screen porch, she plopped down on one and watched as the downpour steadily increased, pummeling the grounds of Belle Coeur until large puddles appeared on the luscious green grass. A cool breeze wafted through the thick screening of the porch, whipping her hair around her face.

The drop in temperature was a blessed relief. She was tired of being hot and sticky. The threat of rain had been in the air for days, but nothing had come of it until dawn, when she woke to the sound of the first light drops against her bedroom window. Now it was coming down hard, the blistering heat finally washed away by the storm.

Thank God. She welcomed it gladly.

Like the impending weather, she had been waiting for something for days, only to be disappointed time and time again when what she thought would happen didn't.

She glanced at her watch. Nine o'clock in the morning and she hadn't seen Sam yet. He hadn't come over the past few days. He'd called her a few days ago and told her he had TNT business to deal with out of town and he would be away for awhile. It was doubtful he would be here today, considering the rain.

She missed him. Damn it all, she didn't want to, but she did. They hadn't said more than a couple polite sentences to each other since that night on Maggie's Bluff. There was never an opportunity to invite him to dinner, a movie, or anything. And then he was gone. It almost seemed as if he was deliberately trying to avoid her.

Well what did she expect? She'd slammed him hard that night. Bruised his ego, telling him that what had happened meant nothing to her. What a lie that was! He made her hotter than the awful humidity that had been hanging around. Hotter than Magnolia's summer.

The truth was, since that night, she realized she wanted more. She didn't want to think beyond that wanting, didn't want to imagine the things she was imagining. Like a future, a home, even a couple of kids. That wasn't her dream; it was someone else's.

Her dream hadn't changed since high school. And it never would. Every day she kept reminding herself that.

All she really needed was sex. Hot, sweaty, wild, no-strings fucking. Just a little time with Sam to burn up the mattresses before she went back to New York.

That's all she needed. Nothing more.

"Morning."

She jumped up and whirled around at the sound of Sam's deep voice. With the rain coming down so hard she hadn't heard him come in the front door.

God he looked good. He wore dark blue jeans and a white T-shirt, soaked from head to foot, dripping water all over her kitchen floor and grinning at her with a devilish smile.

Her body thrummed to life with renewed passion. He looked edible and sexy as hell.

For the first time in days, she smiled. "Morning to you too. Need a towel?"

"Yeah. Sorry about the floor," he said as he tried not to move. "Didn't realize I was so wet."

She grabbed a towel from the laundry area off the kitchen and he dried his hair and arms. Then he took off his shirt to dry his chest and back. The sight of his bare chest made her heart thump heavily and her mouth went dry.

Dark curls spread from the bottom of his neck all the way to the waistband of his pants. And lower. She wanted nothing more at the moment than to slowly trail her fingers through the hair on his chest. And lower. Much lower.

Then follow the same trail with her tongue until she reached his shaft.

"See something you want?"

Her face warmed as her gaze flew up from his crotch to his face. He had caught her ogling his chest and belly. And lower.

"Uhh..." *Speak you dolt. Say something, anything to change the subject.* "Want some coffee?"

He laughed and went to grab a cup from the cupboard. "Sure. I can help myself."

Idiot. She was mortified at having been caught peeking like a teenager. As if she'd never seen a man's naked chest before. Actually, she'd never seen a chest quite like Sam's before.

"Did you get your business taken care of?" She tried to keep her mind, and her eyes, off his chest.

"Yeah, sure did. I'm ready to go back to work on the house now."

Taking a quick glance outside at the continuing downpour, she asked, "How are you going to manage that today?"

He looked up at the ceiling, obviously checking for roof leaks. "Thought I'd start work inside."

"Oh." Inside. Where she was going to be all day, since there were no rehearsals. She intended to work on the script and production notes. Now she had to contend with Sam being underfoot all day. Around her, near her, all day long. Hopefully with a shirt on, or she'd certainly get nothing done.

"Is that a problem?"

"Uhh, no that'll be fine. I was intending to work at home today, too. Will I be in your way?"

He shook his head. "Nope. Not in the least. It's a big house. I'm sure we can stay out of each other's way."

Out of each other's way her foot. Every time she turned around, Sam was right there. Not watching her, not like she was watching him. His gaze focused only on his work, instead of on her.

At least he had the decency to put another shirt on. A dry shirt. A dry, gray, tight across his chest, sleeveless T-shirt. He'd also changed from his tight jeans into very loose shorts. Shorts with holes. Those kinds of shorts a woman would throw away when her man wasn't looking. The kind that hid very little.

And for God's sake, did the man have to work on a ladder, so close to where she was sitting? How could she possibly hope to focus on her work when she was forced to spend all her time gazing at Sam's magnificent ass?

"What do you think of it?" he asked, his voice startling her.

"Huh?" What did she think of what—his ass?

"Come here. I'll show you."

Jordan placed her notes aside and stepped to the ladder. He was inspecting something on the wall.

"Do you think it matches?"

She had no idea what he was talking about. "Do I think what matches?"

"The paint. I thought the original color was eggshell, but now it doesn't seem the same."

"I can't tell from down here."

"Well, come up here and look." He climbed down from the ladder, and held it steady for her.

Had she noticed before the flecks of green in his turquoise eyes? She stared into them, hoping for some reaction. But Sam was obviously preoccupied with house repairs and didn't have his mind on her. Which was annoying because *she* sure as hell was distracted.

"Get up there and look closer, then tell me what you think."

Tentatively, she climbed the first few steps of the ladder. Heights were not her favorite thing, and she was never comfortable on ladders. They always seemed so unstable. But not wanting to appear like a citified sissy, she climbed up anyway.

The ladder shook, and she held on for dear life.

"It's okay, sugar, I've got you," he said as he steadied the ladder with his foot, and then climbed on the bottom rung and held on to her hips. "How's that?"

Nice. Very nice. Strong, warm hands gripping her hips, gently but firmly. Very, very nice. If she turned around, his face would be level with her—

"Jordan."

"Hmm?"

"Are you listening to me? I said, what do you think?"

What she thought was how nice it would be to spend the afternoon having Sam kiss her, touch her and make love to her.

"That would be nice," she responded.

"What would be nice?"

"What?"

"Jordan, are you okay? You haven't heard a word I've said in the past two minutes."

Oh damn. He had been talking? She was daydreaming. About sex. Hot, sweaty, passionate, do-it-right-here-right-now sex.

"Sorry," she said, shaking the visuals from her mind. "I was thinking about production notes." *Big, fat, liar.*

"Let's try this again. Look at the paint I just applied. Now look at the portion of the wall that hasn't been painted yet. Does it match close enough? And if it doesn't, do you like the original color, or the new?"

Concentrate, girl. You can do this. She inspected the two colors, and noticed no discernible difference whatsoever. But then she wasn't the expert.

"Sam, it looks so close I can't tell the difference. Either way, paint it with the new color. It looks fine."

"That's what I needed to know. Thanks." Sam pulled her away from the ladder abruptly and she couldn't help but squeal in shock. Laughing at her, he swooped her up in his arms and cradled her against his chest. Feeling a bit unsteady, she wrapped her arms around his neck for added support.

Big mistake. The heat of his body burned through her shorts and halter-top, lighting a fire within her that nothing but the touch of Sam's lips to hers could extinguish. The amused look suddenly left his face, and his eyes smoldered with the same fire that was raging through her body.

His face was so close that with the barest of movements, their lips could touch. If she just leaned toward him a bit—

Suddenly she was upright and Sam released her.

"Thanks," he said, the fire in his eyes completely extinguished. He turned away from her and headed back up the ladder. "Sorry to bother you. Now back to work for both of us."

That was it? Hadn't he felt it? The electrical charge, the heat between them when he held her? Jordan could still feel his touch. Her skin was on fire where Sam's arms had held her. And now he was back on the ladder, completely ignoring her.

Dammit! This was frustrating.

* * * * *

All in all it was a great day. Sam managed to accomplish quite a bit around the house, even with Jordan so close. Even now he grinned when he recalled the look on her face after he pulled her off the ladder. Wide-eyed, she was flushed and warm to his touch. Her cheeks reddened, she licked her lips and all but issued a verbal invitation to kiss her.

Damn, he'd wanted to kiss her. That would have only been the start of it. Once he touched his mouth to hers, he knew he'd have been lost. It took every ounce of willpower he possessed to put her down and walk away. He had a lot of experience with women, was pretty adept at knowing when a woman wanted him. Jordan wanted him, as much as he wanted her. But Sam wanted her to have a little more time to think about it. Enough time to ask for what she wanted, rather than him pushing her into it.

How much longer she would wait, he didn't know. How much longer could he stand the torture? Not much longer at all.

Staying away the past few days was much more difficult than he'd thought it would be. Even with TNT business to keep him busy, thoughts of Jordan crept into his mind often during those days. He thought of her expressive face, how it revealed so much about what she was thinking and feeling. The sound of her laughter when she was happy and the sexy way she yelled at him when she wasn't.

At night when he lay alone in his hotel room bed, he remembered the satiny feel of her skin. Softer than any woman he'd been with before, just gliding his fingertips over her was like touching a work of art. And the taste of her mouth, so warm and inviting. And her woman's body, the way she responded when he kissed her, the way he knew she'd respond when he made love to her.

Which he hoped was damn soon because he was getting tired of having a hard-on twenty-four hours a day.

He'd made it a point to work wherever she worked today. If she was in the kitchen, so was he. If she was in the great room, he was there, too. Maybe his plan was driving her wild, but it was also driving him past the point of sanity. He was going to have to leave soon, or he'd be the one begging Jordan to kiss him, pleading with her to let him make love to her.

That wouldn't do at all. This had to be her choice.

After he'd cleaned up the last of his work area, he headed into the great room to tell Jordan he was leaving. He halted at the archway, his next breath caught in his throat.

She was sound asleep on the large sofa, piles of her papers strewn across the floor in front of her. She lay on her side facing him, her knees drawn up against her chest. And she was shivering.

The window in the great room was open, the room significantly cooler now that the rain had brought a cold front through.

God, she was breathtakingly beautiful in sleep. Her face was relaxed, her lips slightly parted, and her breathing steady and even. Her cheeks were flushed despite the cold in the room. A rush of longing nearly buckled his knees. His pulse raced and his dick hardened. At that moment he wanted nothing more than to curl up behind her on the sofa, pull her against him, and stroke every inch of her body. The longing was so intense it took his breath away.

He approached her quietly, picked up a light throw that was lying over the back of the sofa and spread it over her. He started to turn to leave, then stopped when he heard a soft moan. The kind of moan that spoke of need and desire.

Did she want him, even in sleep? Was she dreaming of him right now, or was that just wishful thinking on his part?

He knelt in front of the sofa, watching her sleep. A stray auburn curl lay across her cheek, and he picked it up and tucked it behind her ear. She didn't even budge.

Feeling bolder, he leaned over and placed a light kiss against the pulse in her neck, inhaling her sweet scent. She moaned again, softly this time, but didn't wake.

She looked vulnerable lying there sleeping, so relaxed and oblivious. Sam couldn't seem to move, couldn't make himself get up and leave, wanting only to sit with her until she woke. As he sat there looking at her, he was struck by a wave of tenderness he'd never felt for a woman before. Not even Penny.

He sat back on his heels in shock as the thought slammed into his head the same time it hit his heart full force.

He was in love with her. Despite her best efforts to push him away, Sam had fallen in love with Jordan. Sometimes she irritated him beyond the capability to think. Most of the time she was sarcastic and unpleasant, and thought little of him and of Magnolia. Yet she was also fiercely intelligent, witty, and possessed a great sense of humor when she chose to show it.

To say nothing of the warmth and passion she exhibited with him. A passion he knew she was capable of, even back in high school when he was rocked by that first kiss.

But falling in love with Jordan hadn't been what he planned. Wasn't what he wanted. God help him, now what was he going to do?

* * * * *

Jordan woke with a start and bolted upright. Her brain was fuzzy and she couldn't quite place where she was. She blinked, forcing the dreamy fog from her mind. In the mist of her dreams she and Sam had made love, outside during the rainstorm, fat pellets dropping on their bodies and cooling the heat they generated with their passion.

Damn, she hadn't wanted to wake up. She rubbed the sleep from her eyes and looked around to gather her bearings.

Okay, she remembered now. She'd fallen asleep on the sofa in the great room.

She must have dropped off while reading. How long ago was that? The room had darkened, although whether it was the storm or merely dusk she didn't know. The clock on the mantle indicated six-thirty. Too early for darkness, so the storm must be the cause.

In answer to her silent question, a flash of light caught her eye and she turned to look out the window. She placed her feet under her and pulled the blanket tighter around her shoulders, feeling chilled. Her cotton shorts and halter-top did little to ward off the unexpected drop in temperature.

How did she get the blanket? And where was Sam? Jordan called out but got no response. He must have left. After all, it was late. Ignoring the disappointment, she rose, stretched and went to close the window a little, peering out into the gathering darkness to see the heavy winds blowing leaves off the trees and causing the boughs to dip towards the ground.

She made her way down the hall into the kitchen and started a pot of coffee to help clear the cobwebs from her head. The storm pounded steadily outside, and remembering many stormy nights without electricity as a child, she set about lighting candles throughout the house. Then she'd see about starting dinner, while there was still electricity.

A pounding at the door startled her and she went to see if anyone was there or if it was just the wind. She peeked through the keyhole and spotted a drenched Sam. Hurrying to open the door, she braced it with her body as the wind all but threw him in the house. He grabbed the door from her and forced it closed.

"It's a badass storm out there," he said as he shook his head, sending water droplets flying everywhere around her. "Truck got stuck."

"Why don't you go upstairs and grab a hot shower?" she suggested, noticing he was completely drenched and muddy from head to toe. "I've already got coffee going. Throw your clothes down and I'll wash them." She pushed him up the stairs before he could utter a response.

She poured coffee for both of them and placed Sam's clothing in the wash. Then she remembered he didn't have any other clothes here—what was he supposed to wear while his were drying?

Her answer came in the form of a mostly dry hunk of gorgeous man, wrapped only in one of her large bath towels.

"Sorry. Didn't think I'd need a change of clothes, and since you ripped the others off me this is my only alternative. Unless, of course," he said with a grin and exaggerated hillbilly accent, "Y'all would like me to parade around buck nekkid for ya."

"No, that's okay." Jordan swallowed and tried to avert her eyes from Sam's half-clad body. She couldn't help but steal a few quick peeks as she placed their coffee on the table.

That towel parted in such interesting places.

Well that did it. Visions of Sam standing naked in the kitchen flooded her mind.

And what a vision it was. Strong arms, perfectly chiseled chest, legs like tree trunks and an ass to die for. Now as for the parts of him she couldn't see, well she could conjure up a multitude of vivid images that made her body temperature rise ten degrees.

"Thank you, sugar."

"For what?" For nearly drooling while watching him?

"For the hot coffee and the shower."

"Oh." Okay, maybe he wasn't reading her mind. Good thing. "You're welcome. I couldn't very well let you stand outside my door wet and cold now could I? I wouldn't leave a dog out in this kind of weather."

"Have I just been insulted?" He cocked his head to the side and gave her a goofy grin, making her laugh out loud.

"Not yet. But it's early." Taking a seat at the table, she asked, "What happened out there?"

"Storm's pretty bad. Miller Road's washed out. Thought I could make it across, but the truck got stuck in the water and mud. I worked for a while trying to dig the back end out, but then the wash got too deep. Couldn't call for help because I left my cell phone at the office. So I decided the safest thing to do would be walk back here and wait it out."

He refilled both their cups while Jordan admired his towel-clad backside.

"I called for a tow while I was upstairs drying off, but they said with the washout it would probably be tomorrow before anyone could come by, since the storm is supposed to last all night and dump a ton of rain. So it looks like you're stuck with me. That is," he said with a disarming grin, "If you don't mind me hanging out here for a while."

The thought of being alone with Sam sent nervous flutters sailing through her stomach. But then again, this is what she wanted, wasn't it? To have some time alone with Sam, to pursue their relationship, at least the physical part of it?

She managed an offhanded shrug, although her body was already double pumping adrenaline. "No, Sam, of course I don't mind. I was planning on having dinner. Would you like to join me?"

"I'd love to. I'm ravenous." Judging from the hungry look he gave her, she doubted he was referring to food. The thought caused her heart to quicken its pace.

In an effort to avert her eyes from Sam's half-clad body, she started dinner. She reached into the top of the cupboard for spices, trying to grasp the oregano without having to use a stepstool.

"Let me get that for you," Sam said as he pressed her against the counter. His naked chest brushed against her bare back. She stifled a moan at the unexpected contact, then bit back a gasp as he pressed his towel-clad lower body against her bottom. The towel was getting hard, too, or at least what was underneath had solidified considerably.

It was all she could do not to push back against him to see if she could feel what was hiding under that towel.

And why the hell not? Why not right here, right now? The evidence of Sam's interest wasn't hidden very well, and her panties were soaked, her nipples beading against her cotton halter.

Now was as good a time as any.

But he retreated before she could tell him what she wanted. Disappointment rushed through her. She closed her eyes, and took a few deep breaths to calm the utter frustration. She took a few moments to regain her composure and calm her shaky hands, then finally turned around only to find Sam once again sitting at the kitchen table.

"Thanks," was all she could manage to say.

They drank their coffee and discussed the storm until the sound of a buzzer signaled his clothes were dry. Sam grabbed them and headed upstairs to change, while Jordan continued to mix the dough in preparation for biscuits. She was grateful he'd be fully clothed upon his return. Any more glances at him in that towel and dinner would either burn or take twice as long to cook. She couldn't concentrate with him hanging around her in a half-dressed state.

"Can I help you with anything?" he asked as he reentered the kitchen.

Jordan turned to respond. Oh, this wouldn't do at all.

He *had* dressed. Sort of. He'd put on his jeans but had left the top button undone, and hadn't bothered to don his shirt. And the only thing Jordan could see near the top button of his jeans was tanned skin and a line of dark hair that disappeared inside, hiding the rest of him from view.

Oh Lord. No underwear. She took a deep breath and sighed.

She was in hell.

"Something wrong?" The corners of his mouth twitched. She knew better than to believe the innocent look he was throwing her way. Sam knew exactly what he was doing to her.

She gritted her teeth and tried her best to smile. "No, I'm fine, thank you." He had roughly five more seconds to taunt her with his body and then she was going to pounce on him.

"Smells good in here. What are you cooking?"

Oh I'm just cooking up ten pounds of sexual frustration. Would you like some? "Spaghetti and meatballs with salad and homemade biscuits."

"Sounds great. How about if I help make the salad?"

They worked together in companionable silence. Sam completed the salad, then helped form the meatballs and set them on the stove to cook. He found a bottle of wine while searching through the cupboards, and poured a glass for each of them.

They sat and ate, drinking wine and talking. Jordan was more comfortable with Sam tonight than she'd ever been before. Perhaps it was the wine. She consumed more than she normally would, making her feel warm and a little lightheaded. And then again, maybe it was because she finally stopped running, realizing there was nothing to be afraid of. After all, she had no future with Sam, and whatever happened between them would be temporary.

"Tell me a little more about yourself, Jordan."

"What do you want to know?"

"About your life. Why you left. I'm curious, I guess, since I did the same thing. Except I came back and you didn't. I keep wondering why."

"Many people leave their homes when they grow up, Sam. Not everyone comes back."

"I know that. But your reasons seem to have more to do with trying to run away from something, rather than trying to move toward something."

She toyed with her wineglass, now empty. Sam leaned over and filled it up again.

"Why do you say that?"

"You're afraid."

"No, I'm not." She dropped her gaze to her glass, unwilling to see the truth reflected in Sam's eyes.

"Yeah, you are." Tilting her chin up, he forced her to meet his probing gaze. "It's not a bad thing. We're all afraid of something. It just seems like your fear has to do with Magnolia, and I'm wondering what scares you so much about living here."

"It's not really the town, it's more like the memories."

"Are they that unpleasant?"

"Actually many of them are. Other than Grandma, I don't have many happy memories about growing up in Magnolia."

At his confused frown, she said, "Come on Sam, you know all about my parents. You don't need me to go into the details. Everyone knows the story."

He stared at her for a moment, then rose from the table and grabbed their wine bottle and glasses. "Come with me."

He moved them into the great room, situating them together on the large sofa.

"Not everyone has great parents, Jordan," he said, draping his arm behind her. "That doesn't drive people away. What is it that drove you out of here?"

Her reasons for leaving were no longer as clear as they once were. "Magnolia reminds me of my mother, I guess. Memories of her still linger. It's embarrassing. When I was eighteen, I just wanted to escape the stigma of being Susie Weston's daughter. As I got older, I didn't want to face the memories, so I stayed away."

"You think everyone here judges you because of who your mother was?"

"No, I think everyone believes I'll end up just like her."

As she looked into his eyes, Jordan didn't see condemnation, only compassion.

"Is that why you're afraid of men?" He ran his fingers lightly along her collarbone. Goose bumps broke out along her flesh as he continued to lazily stroke her shoulder and neck.

She stared out the window at the powerful storm. "I'm not afraid of men." Not all men, just men like Sam.

Men she could have feelings for, could care for, could fall in love with. Men who could break her heart.

"You're afraid of me."

"I am not afraid of you."

"Are you afraid of this?" He slid his knuckles lightly up her neck and across her jaw, gently tracing her lips with the tip of his fingers.

"No." Her breathing quickened and her heart began to race.

"How about this?" He leaned in and kissed her collarbone, blazing heat along the way as his lips followed his fingers, stopping at the corner of her mouth. He whispered gently, his breath caressing her cheek. "Are you afraid of this?"

"No." She could barely breathe, her chest rising and falling rapidly with the effort of taking in enough oxygen to fuel her growing desire.

"Then *this* must be what you're really afraid of." He turned her towards him, slid his arms around her back and pulled her close. Their eyes met for the briefest of moments before Sam covered her mouth with his.

Chapter Ten

Thunder rumbled powerfully outside as Sam's demanding mouth claimed hers. Her response was as fierce as the storm, urging him to explore, to plunder, eagerly parting her lips in invitation.

Whether it was the wine or simply the intoxicating kisses Sam rained over her lips and throat she didn't know. All she knew was she felt dizzy, spiraling out of control in a maelstrom of desire and emotion.

He pulled his mouth away, leaning his forehead against hers, his breathing erratic. But still he continued to touch her, caressing her bare shoulders and arms in slow, maddening movements.

"Before we go any further I need to tell you something."

Jordan lifted her head, shocked at the blazing desire she saw reflected in Sam's eyes. "What is it?" She tried to calm her shaking limbs and nervous heart.

He paused, and she went insane. What did he need to tell her? What was so important that he had to stop in the middle of their passion?

He'd changed his mind. That had to be it. Instead of her being the one to pull back, it was going to be Sam. He didn't want her after all.

"I had a secret crush on you in high school."

That wasn't what she had expected to hear. And yet it was the most romantic thing he could have said to her. She felt like a teenager who'd just been asked to go steady for the first time.

"You did?" She was unable to suppress her grin.

He nodded, a wry smile lifting the corners of his mouth. "Big time."

"I never knew."

"I didn't want you to know."

"Why not?"

"I didn't think I was good enough for you."

She was certain the surprise she felt showed on her face. "Why did you think that?"

"You were smart, talented and ambitious. I was a slacker, heading down the wrong road and didn't want to take you with me. Besides," he said with a teasing grin, "You're not my type."

She laughed then. "Oh I'm not, am I?"

"Well, maybe not then."

"What about now?"

The smoldering flame in his eyes told her how he felt.

"I think you already know the answer to that." He dipped his head and pressed his mouth against hers. Jordan gave him entry as his tongue slid between her lips, teasing and tasting.

Something was happening to her, something she had never allowed to happen before. The door to her heart, locked tight all these years, suddenly creaked open and allowed Sam a glimpse inside. The one man she'd dreamed about in all her girlhood fantasies was finally holding her in his arms—kissing, wanting, and needing her as much as she needed him. And she did need him. At this moment, more than she'd ever needed anyone.

She tilted her head as Sam nibbled her neck, eliciting shivers of need throughout her body. Her nipples hardened in response as his tongue danced along the sensitive nerve endings of her throat.

Suddenly he grabbed her and pulled her beneath him on the sofa, climbing on top of her and nestling his hard cock against her sex.

She could go up in flames right this moment. Especially since he was rocking against her inflamed pussy.

Framing her face between his hands, he looked at her, the unmasked desire in his eyes sending tremors coursing through her. He whispered, softly and huskily as his eyes held her transfixed. "Jordan, what do you want to have happen between us tonight?"

He was giving her the choice. Letting her decide what would or wouldn't happen between them. If she wanted to back out, change her mind, this was the time to do it. But did she really want to run again?

It didn't take long to decide. She was through running. Opening the door to her heart, she let Sam in completely. She slid her fingers into his hair and pulled him toward her until their lips were almost touching.

"Make love to me, Sam," she whispered.

His reaction was swift and passionate as he seared her lips with his kiss. She gasped as he pressed his body intimately against hers, letting her know he was ready, willing, and oh-so able to grant her wish.

"We have too many clothes on." He stood and pulled her up with him.

She had to agree. Although the breeze from the open window blew cool air into the room, her body was flushed with heat. And she was ready to feel Sam's naked skin against hers.

He swiftly untied the halter at her neck and back, then pulled away from her, his gaze dropping to her bare shoulders, then settling on her breasts as he pulled the two sides of the halter down.

"You're so beautiful." Sam trailed his fingers over the swell of her breasts, lightly circling her nipples until Jordan gasped. "I've wanted to touch you for so long."

And she had been dying for him to touch her too. For as long as she could remember. Yearned for it, dreamed of it. And now it was happening.

A sudden flash of lightning knocked out the electricity. The candles she'd lit earlier bathed Sam in their warm glow. Tracing his face with her fingertips, she shivered as he rubbed his beard-stubbled chin against her palm, then pulled her hand toward him, placing a light kiss on the inside of her wrist.

Keeping eye contact with her, he traced the swell of her breasts, then laid his hands over them. The calluses on his palms scraped lightly against her nipples as he cupped the swollen globes, the dusky peaks hardening like pebbles. Sweet, delicious sensations pooled deep within her as Sam tortured her with slow, precise movements.

But he wasn't going to be the only one touching. She ran her hands along his shoulders and back, marveling at the muscled softness of his skin. He arched against her palms, groaning as her hands traveled lower, her fingers teasingly dipping inside the waistband of his jeans.

"Shit!" he ground out, reaching for her wrist and yanking it away from his heated cock. "Not yet."

Why couldn't she manage to breathe? "Sam, I want to—"

"I want to see you first," he whispered, his gravelly voice causing spasms of need within her core. "All of you."

She stepped back, allowing him to slide her shorts down over her hips, his hand blazing a sensuous trail over her thighs and buttocks as her clothing dropped to her feet. Jordan reeled in anticipation of what was to come.

"Perfect." His gaze traveled over her naked body, his husky voice and blatant approval tearing away any shred of modesty she may have had.

"Now you." She grasped the zipper of his jeans, reveling in his harsh intake of breath as her knuckles brushed his swollen shaft. Slowly she pulled the zipper down, watching his eyes darken and smolder like the storm-laden clouds outside as she boldly slid her hand inside, cupping his heated length.

"God, Jordan," Sam rasped through clenched teeth. "You make me crazy."

It was all she could do not to throw her head back and howl at the primitive pleasure of touching him so intimately. She pushed the jeans further down and reached for his cock.

So beautiful. Thick, hard, pulsing with life and hot to the touch. She swirled her thumb over the silken fluid gathered at the tip, then drew her thumb to her mouth and tasted him. Sam watched her movements, his chest rising and falling sharply when she licked his essence off her thumb.

Grasping her by the shoulders and moving her backward, he slid his jeans down and off until he stood gloriously naked before her.

He was magnificent. Tall, tanned and muscular, he stood like a Greek statue before her, his arousal bold and compelling. Knowing his desire matched her own stripped any reservations she may have had as she walked confidently into his arms.

It had never been like this for Sam. Not even with Penny, and admittedly the sex with her had been pretty good, even if their marriage hadn't been. But with Jordan it was different.

Was it because he loved her? Maybe. But as he ran his hands over her lush, naked body, feeling her tremble in response, he was overwhelmed.

She was perfection. Not just physically, but in every other way. So giving, so open with him, sharing this most precious of gifts in ways that went far beyond the physical. And doing it all with trepidation, as he knew she had reservations about getting involved with him.

He'd have to banish those reservations, because he wanted her in his life.

He dipped his head and licked her bottom lip. She opened for him and he devoured her. Her mouth was warm, wet and inviting, and tasted like the wine they'd consumed at dinner mingled with the sweetest flavor that was uniquely her own. The way she looked at him and responded to his touch with soft moans and sighs tore him apart inside. The fact that she enjoyed the pleasure he was giving her made him want to give her more.

And her blatant assessment of his masculinity tore at him until he wanted nothing more than to lay her down and plunge deep within her. But he held back, wanting to give her more time. Truthfully, *wanting* to take more time with her.

He pushed the coffee table out of the way with his foot, then threw the large pillows from the couch onto the floor. Adding several blankets to the makeshift bed, he laid her on them and dropped down on the floor next to her, pulling her against his chest.

She sank into his embrace, relaxing and resting her head on his shoulder. Not surprisingly, they fit together perfectly. Her long legs, so smooth and soft, intertwined with his.

For a moment neither of them spoke, and Sam listened to the distant sounds of thunder as the rain continued to come down heavily. The scent of summer filled the air—sweet, pungent flowers and the sharp, heady aroma of wet grass. Lightning arced across the sky, bathing the room in its white-hot glow. A storm of epic proportions was coming.

"Sam?" she asked, her voice barely above a whisper.

"Yeah?"

"Before we go any further there's something I have to tell you."

He smiled lightly, hearing her use the same phrase he had earlier.

"Sure baby, what is it?"

"I haven't done this in awhile."

He grinned in the darkness, pleased with her admission.

"Ditto," he replied as he kissed the top of her head. Jordan's hair smelled like strawberries, mingling with the intoxicating aroma of her passion. She aroused him to new heights until he wanted to breathe her in and taste her everywhere, his desire to please her uppermost in his mind.

From what she'd told him, he'd gotten the idea she'd never really experienced intimacy the way she was supposed to, had purposely chosen men who didn't turn her on.

Maybe he was wrong, but he got the idea he turned her on. And he was about to do a helluva lot more than that.

Her hands inched along his body, fingertips lightly trailing across his chest, over his stomach, and lower. As she touched him she watched his eyes, smiling every now and then as his breathing quickened. The look of complete joy on her face as she explored him was like a fist squeezing his heart.

When she slid her palms lower, grazing her nails over his cock, then pulling back he couldn't stand it any longer.

"Quit teasing. Touch me, Jordan."

The green sparkle in her eyes intensified. She boldly took his shaft in her hands, playing with different speeds and strokes until he groaned out loud, fighting to keep from jettisoning his come onto her fingers. He let her know with his eyes and his moans of pleasure how much he enjoyed the feel of her hands on him, wordlessly encouraging her to continue until he almost reached the breaking point.

Which was right now.

With a quick turn he'd flipped her onto her back. He dipped his head and kissed her lips lightly, then with more fervor as their passion grew. Taking direction from her responses, he tried to give her exactly what she wanted. More when she whimpered, less when she seemed to have trouble catching her breath.

He reveled in her taste, the texture of her lips sliding against his. She was like heaven on earth, his dream come true, and he wanted this moment to last forever.

Jordan was mindless with desire as Sam continued to plunder her mouth while he slowly explored her body with excruciating thoroughness. His hands roamed intimately, followed by his lips as he teased and tasted her flesh, lightly bathing her nipples with his tongue until he pulled the taut buds into his mouth.

"Oh, God," she murmured, clutching at his hair and pulling him closer.

"More?" he mumbled against her breast.

"Yes. More."

He suckled harder, her nipple on fire from his hot mouth, the sensation shooting between her legs and making her throb almost painfully.

Sam gave her so much more than she had ever hoped for. Although she tried not to mix emotion into this, it was a momentous occasion. Where in her past she had given her body, with Sam she gave her heart. The thought both frightened and exhilarated her.

After tantalizing her breasts until she panted with need, he moved up and took her mouth once again, plundering her lips until she was mindless and moaning.

Desire coiled tight in her belly. How could kissing be so erotic? How could she have missed this before? No man had ever made her wet from kissing her, yet every swipe of his soft lips against hers, every time his tongue meshed with hers, her cunt wept its response.

When his hand trailed over her abdomen and lower, she arched her hips and spread her legs, desperate now for what he could give her. He separated the slick folds of her sex and found her clit, stroking it lightly until she gasped, on the verge of tumbling over the edge.

His fingers dipped inside the swollen folds, testing her, stroking slowly over and over until her cream poured over him, telling him without words she was ready.

"Please, Sam," she begged, wanting to feel him inside her, needing the intimacy of his flesh joined to hers more than she ever needed anything before.

"Not yet. I want to watch you come."

Oh, God. She couldn't wait that long. "Fuck me."

"As you wish." But instead of sliding his cock inside her, he stayed where he was, swirling his thumb over her clit and plunging his fingers inside her.

He was relentless, demanding what she didn't want to give. She couldn't. Yet with every stroke he brought her closer and closer. She couldn't escape it if she tried.

"Come on, baby. Let go for me. Come on my hand. Let me feel your cunt squeeze my fingers."

Unable to hold back, she released the tenuous hold on what little control she had left and cried out, arching her back and driving her pussy down over his fingers. Juices poured from her pussy and down her ass, her climax long, hard and eminently satisfying.

He withdrew his fingers, kissed her again, then positioned himself between her legs. Poised above her, he nudged her legs apart with his knee and took his cock in his hand, stroking it slowly, deliberately, capturing her attention with each thrust.

It didn't take long for the throbbing to begin again. Her nipples beaded and she reached for them, plucking the buds until they stood erect and hard, waiting for his mouth to cover them.

With a slow, seductive smile, Sam slid the tip of his arousal inside, his half-lidded eyes locked with hers as that first jolt of intimate connection made her gasp. Her cunt instinctively grasped him, pulling him in until he was fully sheathed.

"Sam," she said breathlessly as she placed her palm on his chest, caressing the soft black curls as he moved within her. His strokes were measured and gentle despite the fast and furious beating of his heart under her hand.

"Yes, baby I know," he replied as he continued his sensuous assault on Jordan's body and heart, compelling both to give all they had. And she did, gladly, pouring forth everything she felt, all that she had never given before.

He quickened his pace at the same time the contractions built to a crescendo inside her, their sweat-slickened bodies moving as one in exquisite harmony.

This was too much to bear. Too intimate, too perfect. She hadn't expected to feel like this...so wanton, so willing to give Sam every part of her. The old fears crept up and weaved their tentacles around her emotions.

"Jordan," Sam said, leaning back to look at her as if he sensed her fear. "Look at me."

She met his gaze and tears filled her eyes. Passion had turned his eyes a stormy blue. His muscles tensed as he rocked against her.

"Lift your hips and fuck me. Give me all of you."

She didn't want to, and yet she wanted to give him all he'd asked of her. Oh, why couldn't she just enjoy this?

"Baby, don't think. Just feel." He shifted, placing his chest against hers, reaching underneath to grab her buttocks. She raised her legs as the contact of his pelvis met her clit. He drove harder, deeper, thrusting until she felt it in her womb.

Don't think, just feel. He was right. This was the moment she'd waited a lifetime for, and she wouldn't let it go.

Clutching desperately at his head, she tugged his face closer, moaning her impending surrender as he led her to a place she had never been, her world colliding and changing as he loved her like she'd never been loved before.

Like the wild and raging storm outside, she was powerless to stop the wind of passion as her climax overtook her. A wailing cry tore from her lips. She clutched fiercely at Sam and lifted her hips to meet his grinding strokes. Pulses of intense pleasure rocketed within her and she let her orgasm gain control. It roared through her like a hurricane wind. Lightning seared the night sky as Sam tumbled with her through the eye of the storm and beyond.

* * * * *

Jordan woke slowly, feeling great even though she'd gotten very little sleep the night before. She stretched, rolled over, and came face to face with her still-sleeping lover.

Lover. The word alone made her giddy as a schoolgirl. She propped her head on her arm and lay still, watching Sam sleep.

Last night had been the most incredible night of her life. Sam surprised her not only with his lovemaking, which admittedly was fantastic, but also his generous nature. The way he normally swaggered around like he was God's gift to women had led her to believe he'd be more interested in his own pleasure than his partner's. But that wasn't the case at all.

They made love several times, and each time he took her to new heights of pleasure. It was as if she was his personal crusade—he wouldn't be satisfied until she was. And man, was she ever! Over and over again.

But there was another element to Sam's lovemaking. Not just physical prowess, but the care he took with her, the way he played with her and teased her. They laughed, they talked, they even wrestled, rolling around on the bed until Jordan had gotten so wrapped up in the covers it took Sam's help to get her out. Which led to another unbelievably erotic session.

It was the first time Jordan had truly enjoyed making love. With the handful of men before Sam it had been a physical release only, because she not only purposely chose men she wouldn't become attached to, she also never gave anyone else what she gave Sam last night.

Her heart.

Then it hit her. Why making love with Sam had seemed so special, so incredibly intimate and emotionally satisfying.

She loved him. She laid her head on her arm and thought about this amazing revelation. It couldn't be love—she was confusing love with sex, with passion. That was it. Rolling over onto her back, she thought about all the reasons she couldn't be in love with Sam Tanner.

He was an opinionated, bull-headed pain in the ass. Sarcastic, arrogant and full of himself. He made her angry more often than not, frustrated her beyond measure, showed up at the most inopportune times, and constantly berated her for choosing New York over Magnolia. She was the proverbial city girl, he the country boy, and never the twain shall meet.

But he was also kind, whip-smart, passionate, an incredible kisser, a wonderful and giving lover and had a wickedly funny sense of humor. The kind of man most women would jump for joy at having for themselves.

Jordan wasn't most women.

That in a nutshell was the problem. She couldn't love him. She had deliberately structured her life not to fall in love, and what did she do? Fell head over heels for the one man she knew was wrong for her.

Okay, she wasn't having any of this love stuff, but maybe she could enjoy the lovemaking. Why not? Men did it all the time, didn't they? Had great sex, then when you gotta go, you gotta go. Isn't that what her father had done to her mother?

"You sure are beautiful in the morning."

She jumped, turning over to find him staring intently at her. Lord, he looked good. Hair sticking out everywhere, the shadow of a beard on his face and a rather prominent erection woke her libido in a savage way.

"How long have you been awake?"

Stretching and rolling on top of her, he cradled her face in his hands and kissed her. "Long enough to see you were deep in thought about something. Long enough to see how beautiful you look with your hair all mussed up." His eyes sparkled with mischief as he turned her head to the side and looked at her throat. "And long enough to spot that huge hickey on your neck."

Her hand flew to her neck. "You're joking, right? You did *not* give me a hickey, did you? Oh shit, I'll be so embarrassed!"

He laughed and kissed her neck. "Just kidding. Remind me to plant one on you sometime, though, just for fun." He gathered her close, then nipped at her collarbone and lower, licking the sensitive spot above her right breast until she struggled to maintain her thoughts.

"But for now," he said as he slid his lips down to tease her already erect nipple, "I'll remember to put love bites in places no one but me can see."

The thought of being branded by him made her shiver, desire springing anew despite the soreness between her legs. A sudden need washed over her — to feel him mark her, to know that she belonged to him, and that he belonged to her.

Ridiculous. Foolish schoolgirl fantasies. Like wearing a guy's class ring. So she never got to experience those things. So what? She was a grown woman now with goals of her own, and those goals didn't include a permanent relationship with Sam Tanner.

Why can't you just enjoy the moment, Jordan? Quit thinking so much.

Forcing thoughts of relationships aside, she focused instead on the goose bumps caused by Sam's thorough attentions. He kissed her neck, her shoulder, nibbling lightly. His hands cupped her breasts, tugging at her nipples until she whimpered, fire burning low in her belly.

God, she was easy. A few kisses and sweeps of his hand over her body and she was ready for him. Eager for him. Nearly desperate to feel him inside her again.

"Tell me what you want, Jordan."

Her gaze met his, loving the fire in his eyes. Tell him what she wanted? There wasn't enough time in the world for that. She wanted so much. Too much.

"Make love to me."

He grinned. "I kinda figured that out already. How do you want it?"

Oh, God. Don't ask her that. "Um, the regular way."

He laughed and licked her bottom lip. "You want it on your knees, or maybe standing up? How about sitting up together. There's a rocking chair over there I'd like to try out sometime."

So many visuals, all conjuring up erotic games and intense sexual play. Yes, she wanted it all. But not right now. "I don't want to think anymore, Sam. Just fuck me."

His grin turned her on more than anything. Wicked, filled with the promise of giving her more than what she could ever imagine.

"Your wish is my command."

He moved above her, taking her hands in his and raising them over her head. Positioning himself between her legs, his gaze captured hers at the moment he plunged into her. She gasped with pleasure at his dominating entry, swept away in a tide of incredible sensations.

"Your pussy was made for my dick," he said, holding tight to her wrists, controlling every one of their movements. "Slick, hot, wet, it squeezes me so damn hard I could come the minute I enter you."

His words, so dark and sensuous, poured over her like an inferno, scorching her, making her want and need only him. A very potent and dangerous man, and yet she couldn't resist him.

Whatever his magic, she wanted more of it. Every day. For—

Forever.

"I've wanted to be inside you so long I couldn't see straight." He continued to drive relentlessly, his balls banging against her ass. When he pulled her upright and turned her onto her belly, she arched her back and waited.

"You have one pretty ass, Jordan," he said, smacking one cheek until it stung. A quite pleasurable sting, too. Gripping her hips, he drove deep, holding himself in check and grinding against her. "I want to fuck your ass, feel it squeeze my cock tight."

Oh God. The images came catapulting at her, one right after the other. Her body open and ready for him, well lubricated so that he could slide his cock deep into her anus. She could actually feel the intensity of the experience.

"Would you like me to fuck your ass, baby?"

So intimate, so personal. Yet something she'd fantasized about time and time again. She didn't even hesitate before answering, "Yes."

His fingers bit into the flesh of her hips as he reared back and thrust harder. She felt the tension coiling inside her, ready to burst. When he leaned over her back and searched between her legs, finding and strumming her clit, she let the tidal wave flow.

Her orgasm overcame her almost immediately. Sam plunged repeatedly inside her, taking her higher than she thought she could go.

"That was a good come," he said, leaning over to nuzzle her neck. She half turned to see him grinning at her like a madman. "Now we're gonna take you there again. Only this time, I'm taking that sweet ass of yours."

Lifting her hips in the air, he slipped a couple pillows under her abdomen.

When he eased a finger inside her slit, she jerked, still feeling the tremors of her prior orgasm. When he withdrew, she heard the sucking sounds, knew he tasted her cream. She'd never heard anything more erotic, or more stimulating.

"Creamy, salty and sweet. Damn, woman, you make me crazy."

She was the one who was crazy. Sam was more than she could ever handle. She wasn't prepared for someone with such a powerful sexuality. She felt inept and completely out of control.

"I love fucking you, Jordan." He thrust his cock inside her again, this time reaching underneath to massage her clit. Seemingly relentless, he led her to the brink again and again, his strokes sure and steady.

He withdrew, petting her slit and taking the juices that poured there to coat her anus. The feel of his fingers stroking there made her quiver with anticipation. She'd often fucked herself in the ass with her toys, but she'd never allowed a man there.

Until now. Now she wanted it, with the only man she could ever imagine taking her this way.

"I have another confession to make."

Jordan stilled, feeling exposed and vulnerable in this position. What could he possibly need to confess to her at this moment? "What is it?"

"I watched you the day you fucked yourself in your room."

Her belly recoiled in panic. "What? When?"

"Not too long ago. You were up in your room, fucking yourself in the ass with a dildo."

Oh, God. How embarrassing. Heat filled her and she was glad she wasn't in a position to look him in the eyes. "How did you... I mean I was alone..."

"I went up on the scaffold to retrieve my tools and I saw you. Your window was open."

"Oh my God. And you watched?"

He caressed her buttocks, his fingers teasing the opening to her anus. "Yeah, how could I not watch? You were so fucking hot, Jordan. My dick was on fire. Hell, I took it out and jacked off while you masturbated."

"You did?"

"Hell, yeah. I had to bite my lip to keep from groaning out loud when I came."

That sent heat spiraling through her womb, her pussy flooding with arousal.

"You just got wetter, baby. Does thinking about that day turn you on?"

As he said the words he slipped the tip of his finger into her anus. She moaned, arching her ass higher.

"Hang on tight, baby," he said, moving off the bed and opening the drawer to her nightstand. "I figured you had to keep it close. Nice toy drawer, by the way. Remind me to use some of those on you."

She laughed, squealing when he poured the cold lube between the cheeks of her ass.

"Nice and slick. It'll be easy for me to slide my dick right in that tight hole."

He probed with the head of his cock, gently pushing forward. More than used to having something in her anus, she lifted, eager to feel a hot cock in there instead of a lifeless jelly plug.

"Ready for it?" he asked, his voice tight.

"Yes. Fuck me, Sam."

He spread her buttocks and slid inside, past the tight barrier. A sharp, tingling pain, but more pleasure than she had ever known before. She cried out and pushed against him, taking his shaft all the way in.

"God, that's so tight." He moved back and pulled partway out, then slid fully inside her again, developing a rhythm. He was gentle with her, obviously not wanting to hurt her, but she needed more.

"Harder."

"Christ, Jordan. You amaze me." He gave her what she asked for, pulling back and driving hard. The pain was intense, the pleasure more so. She never knew that being fucked in the ass could be so incredibly arousing.

"Reach underneath and touch your clit for me. I want you to come again."

She did as he asked, finding her clit, using her other hand to plunge her fingers inside her pussy.

"Oh, yeah," he said, thrusting hard. "Fuck your pussy for me. Come for me."

"I can't do this," she cried, unable to deal with the never-ending tension and release.

"Yes, you can. Give it to me, baby."

She tossed her head from side to side. Pleasure washed over her again, shocking her. She'd thought she had no more to give until Sam coaxed her towards the summit one last time.

She felt the tightening and strummed her clit in rhythm to Sam's strokes, drawing closer and closer to an explosion.

"I'm gonna come," he said, his body tightening against her, his cock twitching. He drove harder, his balls slapping against her.

Jordan lost it then, bucking her ass against him and crying out as she climaxed, flooding her hand with her juices. Sam groaned and shoved deep, his hot cream filling her anus as he jerked repeatedly.

She lay there, panting, still feeling the tingling aftershocks of her orgasm.

He withdrew and helped Jordan up, then pulled her into the shower with him, soaping her body tenderly, turning her every few seconds for a soul-shattering kiss. They dried off and he led her to the bed, gathering her close to his chest and stroking her wet hair. She listened to the sound of his heart, knowing by his rhythmic breathing that he had drifted off.

More content than she had any right to be, she let herself fall into oblivion, both in awe and scared to death that she had just bitten off way more than she could chew.

Chapter Eleven

The days passed like a blur of nonstop momentum. Jordan busily prepared the production for the Summer Festival, less than a week away. The cast was well rehearsed and ready. A buzz had already started about the musical, many people telling her they anticipated it as the social event of the summer.

She had to admit she was getting a bit excited too. To be completely in charge of a production was something she'd been aching to do for years, but with the size of the theater in New York she hadn't yet been given the opportunity to run her own show. At best she was an assistant to the producer and directors of whatever shows were booked at the theater. This production, from virtually the beginning, was hers to run. And she loved it, even if it was a small-town affair.

In the meantime, Sam was finishing up the house. The ceilings and walls were all repaired and repainted. The outside of the house bore a fresh coat of paint and the roof had been replaced so there would be no more water leaks. She had to admit he was doing a great job.

She watched him one day when he brought in his crew to help. Sam was, without a doubt, the man in charge. He barked orders, climbed all over scaffolds and rigging like Tarzan, and without a care for his own safety made sure the job was done right.

Her heart skipped several beats as she watched him move around on the scaffolding. Not only was he in complete command of his physical abilities, he also managed a crew quite well. He spoke with authority and commanded respect, and they gave it to him easily because they knew he was willing to do the same work they were doing, without fear or complaint. She could see the respect his employees gave him, and admired him for that.

Of course Jordan also enjoyed watching him work, whether alone or with a crew. Because the weather was so hot and humid, he usually worked in shorts and no shirt, muscles rippling as he hammered or painted.

She had to admit she found herself coming up with a myriad of excuses to be near him, whether to inspect the work being done, or bring him a glass of iced tea during the hot hours of the afternoon. Invariably she ended up staying, talking with him about any and all subjects as he worked and she watched.

Typically they discussed either the house or the play. Occasionally Sam made Jordan laugh with town gossip, like the fact that Josiah Edmunds, barely eighteen years old, had been caught by his father, Donald, banging the twenty-three year old high school English teacher in his father's house.

Jordan was appalled, but Sam just laughed. He explained it wasn't that Donald was angry about his son becoming a man with an older woman, but the fact that said older woman was also Donald's girlfriend at the time.

Which Jordan found even more shocking. But then Sam informed her that Donald received another blow to his already fragile ego when the English teacher said she preferred the son over the father, and promptly skipped town with her new young stud, leaving Donald minus both a son and a girlfriend. Sam said Donald would probably not mourn the loss for long, as he'd recently been spotted hanging out at the bowling alley ogling one of the young barmaids who had to be at least twenty years his junior.

No doubt about it. The gossip in a small town was infinitely more detailed and interesting than one would be privy to in a large city, where most people kept their private lives private. Private wasn't even a word in Magnolia's dictionary.

Besides their work, Jordan and Sam found ample time to play. They made love at every opportunity. In the mornings before she left for town, and on the days she worked at home at almost every break Sam took. She teased him that she was glad she wasn't paying him by the day, because she'd feel cheated. Sam laughed and told her she was getting more than her money's worth out of him, as stud service wasn't included in their original contract.

She pulled in front of the house, still amazed at the changes that had taken place in just a few short weeks. Before, the house had been in a state of disrepair. Now it shined like new. So new, in fact, that the realtor she had spoken to when she first came to town finally placed a *For Sale* sign in the front yard, deeming it ready to show.

The sign glared at her like an ugly reminder of what she was doing. A pang of regret hit her, which she quickly brushed aside as she walked up the stairs to the front door. She refused to deviate from her goals. Her dream was in reach and she wasn't going to change her mind.

It was late, but Sam must still be working since his truck was parked out front. She wondered what he could be doing this time of night. He'd told her he didn't want to paint in the evenings because the light of day was better to ensure an even application of color.

As she opened the front door she took a deep breath. The house smelled like lavender. Dusk had settled over the house, indicating the need for lights, but none were on. Instead, small purple candles lined every step of the staircase leading upstairs, the tiny votives providing the explanation for the lavender smell.

Music was playing on the second floor—soft jazz, sensual and enticing. Smiling, she took each step, following the trail of candlelight like a roadmap. She hummed in tune to the music, her body swaying in rhythm to the slow, seductive blends of saxophone and piano.

At the top of the stairs the candles continued to light her way, glowing like a runway on each side of the hallway, leading into her bedroom. She followed them as well as the music, breathing deeply of their sweet aroma.

She entered her bedroom and stopped. No sign of Sam, but there were candles lit everywhere—on her dresser, both nightstands, and the windowsill. There were no lights on in here either, and the candlelit illumination across her bedroom was incredibly romantic. Then something on the bed caught her eye.

A soft sigh of pleasure escaped her lips as she spied a small bunch of violets on her pillow, neatly tied with a ribbon. Her heart lurched and she fought back tears as she picked them up and inhaled their sweet scent.

Where did the man find time to do these things, taking such care to set a romantic scene for her, and still manage to work on the house? She was overcome by the obvious care Sam had taken to fill her room with scents, flowers and music, suddenly anxious to find him.

The music was coming from her bathroom, sexy jazz that slid under her skin like warm brandy on a snowy night. She followed the sound and her heart stopped when she pushed the door open.

The bathroom was aglow in candlelight. In every available space, lavender candles filled the room. The scent was intoxicating. Candles surrounded the oversized tub in the corner of the room, which was filled almost to the rim with water, bubbles and one very sexy looking man.

She smiled and shook her head. One very sexy, very obviously naked, very hot-looking man sitting in a bath of bubbles, surrounded by lavender candles and soft music. Only a man confident enough in his masculinity would be comfortable with bubble bath and candlelight.

Sam was one confident man.

"Thought maybe you'd like a bath, some music and a glass of wine," he said, his smile lighting her own as he held up a glass for her. "And of course, your own personal masseur to work away any tension in your shoulders...or wherever."

As she walked toward the tub, she began to slowly unbutton her sleeveless blouse. "Masseur, huh?" She watched his eyes devouring every buttonhole she opened. "Sounds like just what I need."

"Baby, I know exactly what you need." His face gleamed in the candlelight as his hot gaze poured over her. Her body burned with desire, loving the fact she could tell by his look he wanted her as much as she wanted him.

Her body flared to life, her breasts swelling, her nipples hardening and her pussy moistening. With one look she was ready for him.

She peeled off her blouse, thankful she'd worn something sexy this morning—a blue silk camisole that hugged her breasts. She slid the skirt down over her hips and stood there under Sam's scrutiny clad in only the silk camisole and matching string bikini.

"Shuck them duds, baby," he said in his sexy southern voice, "and get in here with me. Now." He smiled, a wicked glint in his eyes that held the promise of things to come.

But good things were worth waiting for. And she felt like teasing Sam a little tonight. Ever so slowly, she drew the camisole down her arms, letting it rest at the top of her breasts.

"Go on," he said, his voice tight as he sipped his wine, his gaze focused on her impromptu striptease.

"Oh, I'll get to it, sugar," she replied in her own sexiest southern accent. The look he gave her was dangerous—impatient and demanding. She knew what he wanted. But she was going to make them both wait for it.

A delicious shiver passed through her as she peeled the camisole the rest of the way down until it pooled at her feet. Sam's blatant assessment of her body was as exciting as if he'd touched her. Then his gaze moved lower, resting on her tiny blue silk panties for a brief second before he looked up again, the passion reflected in his hot looks causing her pulse to skitter rapidly.

"Get 'em off, Jordan, and fast, because I want you in here with me now."

Still playing, she hesitated, smiling mischievously as she stood a few feet away from the tub, chewing her bottom lip as if trying to decide if she'd actually get in the bath with him or not.

His hot look burned her to the spot, those gorgeous turquoise eyes storming with desire. "I'm warning you. My patience is running thin. Get those panties off while they're still in one piece, or I'll get up and rip them off."

Ripples of excitement coursed through her at his sensual threat. Flashing him a devilish smile, she trailed her fingers lightly around the skimpy strings on her hips, and then dipped one hand inside, teasing him to the breaking point.

"That does it!" He shot out of the water, standing there for a millisecond, dripping wet, gloriously naked, his erection prominent. His eyes gleamed dangerously as he stepped quickly out of the tub and in two strides had her in his arms. His mouth came down hard on hers as he ravaged her with his tongue, and at the same time turned her silk panties into shreds and swept her into his arms.

Words weren't necessary as they frantically clutched at each other, passion overcoming any desire for slow, languorous lovemaking. That would come later. Right now, she wanted him. No foreplay, no more teasing. Just wanted him inside her.

"Now, Sam, hurry," she pleaded.

He pushed her against the bathroom wall and cupped her bottom in his hands, lifting her off the ground. She held on to his shoulders and wrapped her legs around his waist as he plunged inside her.

Their coupling was fast and furious, both of them already hot and ready. Sam plundered her mouth, hard and demanding, and she gave in return, digging her nails into his shoulders and crying out as release came fast.

He groaned against her mouth, not pausing in his thrusts, just pressing against her and grinding against her clit. She splintered into a million pieces again, crying out as the waves of pleasure washed over her. His fingers dug into the soft flesh of her buttocks as he yelled with the force of his release.

They regained their breath slowly, still joined and unable to move. Jordan laid her head on Sam's shoulder, kissing his damp skin until he lowered her feet to the floor.

"Ready for that bath now?" he said, grinning like the well-satisfied man that he was.

"I think we both need one." She laughed, sliding her sweat-slickened breasts against his chest.

Sam scooped her up in his arms and stepped into the bath. He sat her down in the water and slid in behind her. She relaxed against him as he handed her a glass of wine and took a sip from his own.

"So, how was your day, dear?"

She giggled. "Fine, darling, and yours?"

"Oh, it was fine. Actually I have good news for you."

Half turning, she looked at him. "Really? What kind of good news?"

"I'm finished."

"Finished with what?"

"The house. Everything is done. Did a once-over at the end of the day to make sure nothing was left unfinished, and it all checked out. My work here is finished."

"Oh." She turned around again and leaned her head against Sam's chest. Sipping her wine, she pondered the disappointment stabbing at her. Sam would no longer be around every day. The thought of not seeing him made her ache with a sense of loss.

"That should make you happy, babe. The job is finished earlier than we anticipated. Now you won't have to worry about trying to get it on the market while it's still being repaired."

"Actually, it's already on the market. Didn't you see the sign in the front yard? Mavis Riley came by the theater earlier this week and said she looked the place over and it appeared ready to sell, so she posted the sign this morning."

"I see. No, I didn't notice it. I was inside all day and I guess I didn't hear her come by." He dipped a sponge in the scented water and squeezed it over her neck and shoulders, causing rivulets to run over her collarbone and chest. "You're closer than ever to getting the property sold. It's prime land and a beautiful house. It should sell quickly."

"I guess so." She couldn't shake the emptiness as she thought about selling the house. It was the closest place to a home she'd ever had. Hell, it was her home.

And she had to admit that living here the past few weeks felt more like home than her apartment in New York ever had.

"Something wrong?" Sam gently massaged the knots newly forming in her shoulders. "You seem tense."

"No, I'm fine," she lied. She wasn't. The house was finished, would most likely be sold soon, and she wouldn't be seeing as much of Sam anymore. And she wasn't one damn bit happy about any of it.

Funny how things could change in a few short weeks. When Jordan first arrived, all she wanted was to sell the house as fast as possible, and keep Sam away from her. Now the opposite was true. She wanted him around — all the time, and wasn't at all happy about the possibility of selling the house.

This was a fine mess. Now what was she going to do?

Her thoughts scattered as Sam licked the side of her neck, eliciting a delicious shiver.

"Cold?" he asked in between nibbles.

"No, not cold at all." She turned her head to the side, allowing Sam better access to her neck.

"Hmm, I think maybe you like this." He kissed her neck, then along her throat toward the back, nipping lightly at her nape with his teeth.

She moaned and pressed against him. He bit harder this time, growling as he tasted her flesh. God, that was so erotic.

"Sam, make love to me," she said breathlessly. "Now."

He stood and scooped her into his arms, taking her, dripping wet, to the bed. He pulled her on top of him and, capturing her face between his hands, pulled her to his lips.

She moved restlessly against him as his hands roamed over her. She wanted him again, wanted to eradicate the sense of loss she felt at his imminent departure from her home, from her life.

There was a desperation in her every move. She knew it, but could do nothing to stop it. If Sam was aware of it, he said nothing, instead taking his time to touch her, kiss her, lift her hips and thrust slowly inside her as if they had all the time in the world.

"That's it," he urged, grasping her hips and lifting her up and down on his shaft. "Ride me, baby. Fuck my cock."

She did, rubbing her clit against him, taking him in deep only to rise and begin all over again. Splinters of need filled her, a desperate urge to feel him inside every part of her.

It seemed as if each kiss, each caress, would be the last. The last time she'd press her mouth to his, the last time they'd join as one. And she needed this joining, now more than ever.

It built quickly inside her, this maddening crescendo of pleasure. Like climbing a mountain and enjoying every step of the way, she luxuriated in each stroke, each kiss, burning his touch into her memory banks forever.

"Touch me, Sam," she pleaded, arching her back and giving him access to her sex.

He reached out, circling her clit, rubbing his fingers back and forth over her swollen pearl until she shrieked with sheer pleasure.

They reached the pinnacle at the same time, once again losing control as she was swept away by emotions and sensations that only confirmed her love for Sam.

Afterward they lay together on her bed. She rested on top of him contentedly as he lazily stroked her back and bottom. They were still intimately connected, neither wishing to break the bond.

Jordan was completely satiated, thoroughly confused, and more than a little afraid. Try as she might to push her feelings for Sam aside, she knew this was much more than a sexual fling.

The ache she felt in her heart when she realized her time in Magnolia would soon be drawing to a close elicited a sadness she had never felt before. Her love for Sam was growing, despite her firm resolve to avoid her feelings for him.

Jordan was one hundred and fifty percent completely crazy in love with Sam Tanner. In a short time she'd be heading back to New York, leaving him behind. The thought of it hurt so bad she wanted to curl up and cry.

And she had no earthly idea what she was going to do about it.

* * * * *

Sam cradled Jordan in his arms, rubbing her back while she drifted off to sleep, exhausted from their multiple lovemaking sessions.

She continued to amaze him, this woman he loved. Her fire and passionate nature equaled his and in her he'd found his perfect partner. But he didn't think she realized that yet.

Tonight he wanted to tell her he was in love with her, but for some reason couldn't bring himself to do it. Maybe it was the old fear resurfacing, the feeling he just wasn't good enough for her. But in whose eyes? Hers, or his?

As far as he knew, she still intended to go back to New York when the house was sold. He thought he sensed some hesitation and disappointment in her voice today when he told her the house was finished and ready to go on the market. But was it really there, or did he just want her to be upset about it?

So upset that maybe she'd change her mind about selling. And about leaving Magnolia.

Of course, he hadn't really given her a reason to stay. He hadn't told her how he felt. Maybe that would change her mind. Then again, maybe it wouldn't.

The thought of losing Jordan was almost more than he could bear. He had to give it his best shot. Tell her what was in his heart, ask her to stay, and then see if what he offered her was worthwhile enough for her to give up her lifelong dream and stay in Magnolia with him.

But was that fair? To ask her to give everything up just to stay here with him?

Of course it wasn't. He could move to New York, too, if she'd have him.

And do what? Be miserably unhappy the rest of his life? No, that he wouldn't do. He'd ask her to stay, fair be damned.

He needed her, loved her, and wanted her to stay. Now he just had to convince her that's what she wanted, too.

Chapter Twelve

The Summer Festival began that morning with a parade through town, although for the life of her Jordan didn't know where all the spectators came from. Almost everyone who lived in Magnolia had a role in the parade, either as a participant, a judge or a decorator.

Family members lined the street to catch glimpses of their loved ones in the parade. It was a small town after all, and trophies were given for just about anything, from floats to the local bands to kids on decorated bicycles, their paper and plastic streamers flying behind them.

She'd been up hours before the parade started, arriving at the theater before dawn to put everything in place for tonight. Despite her self-reassurance that this was no big deal, the butterflies flitting around her stomach were just as big as if she were opening a play on Broadway tonight.

She took a break from last-minute preparations for the play to step outside and view the mile-long line of bands, floats, civic groups and miscellaneous entries making their way down Main Street in front of the theater.

A childlike enthusiasm filled her as she watched clowns tossing candy to the crowds of excited children lined up along the parade route. Squeals of delight were heard for blocks at the appearance of the local high school floats, a perennial favorite among the town. There was always a fierce competition as each grade level tried to outdo the other and win the prized Best High School Float award.

"You look like a kid."

Jordan jumped as Sam snuck up behind her.

"You scared me!" she protested, pushing half-heartedly against him. "Quit sneaking up on me!"

Laughing, Sam pulled her against his chest and wrapped his arms around her waist as they watched the parade. "I didn't sneak up on you at all. Admit it. You were so enthralled with this small-town hokey parade that you wouldn't have noticed if the Queen of England stepped in front of you."

She giggled. "Maybe."

"Maybe my ass." He brushed a light kiss on the side of her neck. She shivered as his warm breath caressed her, and for a moment thought of other things besides the parade. Things equally exciting, but for an entirely different reason.

Leaning against Sam and watching the parade snake through town, she felt a sense of rightness she hadn't felt for years. And also a sense of foreboding. This wasn't supposed to be happening. It wasn't what she planned. But it happened anyway.

Little by little, she was falling in love with her hometown again, and had already fallen hard for Sam. Although she knew she'd be leaving soon, she hadn't quite figured out what she'd do when the time actually came to go.

Face it Jordan. You're a procrastinator of the worst sort, and too much of a coward to face how you really feel and deal with it.

"I love you, Jordan."

She froze, barely breathing.

Surely she'd imagined what she'd just heard. Had Sam just whispered that he loved her? Had she heard him right? Her heart pounded and her palms grew sweaty.

She turned and looked at him. There was something different in his eyes. Subtle, but there nonetheless. A warmth, a light, those ocean blue eyes glowing with something she hadn't seen there before.

Love. Sam *loved* her. Good God, what was she going to do?

But did he really? Or was she just seeing what she wanted to see in his eyes? The old uncertainty came back to haunt her, the doubt that never really went away. Her mother had thought the same thing—that her father loved her. She had been wrong. Maybe Jordan was too. But why would Sam say it if he didn't mean it?

Oh, why couldn't she just believe him? Why couldn't she trust in him, and in herself? Why always the doubt?

He loved her. He said it so he must mean it. What would it mean for the two of them? And her dream? Was it changing, did she now want something different?

Should she tell him she loved him too? That was scary, admitting that you loved someone. She'd never done it before, had never felt it before. Now that she did, she really wanted to tell him.

She started to speak but Sam placed a finger against her lips, silencing her.

"Don't say anything, it doesn't require a reply. I've wanted to tell you for some time now, and I know this isn't the most romantic place to do it, but I feel it and it's out there and that's all you need to know." He took her chin in his hand, raised her face up to his and planted a kiss on her lips so gentle and sweet it almost made her cry.

Then he smiled at her. God how she could get lost in that smile.

"Go do what you need to do. You've got a very busy day. We'll have time later to talk. Oh I forgot," he added with a huge grin, "Break a leg tonight, babe."

He'd put it out there. And she would too. Then they'd talk, decide what was going to happen next. She vowed to tell him tonight what was in her heart. As she watched him walk away, she whispered, "I love you too, Sam. God help me, but I love you too."

* * * * *

The play was a huge success. It was a perfect July evening, a slight breeze keeping everyone cool.

Having the performance outside at the local park provided enough space for everyone to attend. And, Jordan noted from the size of the crowd, surely the entire town had been present for Magnolia's first community theater event.

They laughed, they cheered, and the cast received three curtain calls. The music was superb. The Magnolia orchestra, a ragtag team of anyone in town who could play a musical instrument, didn't miss a note and accompanied the singers to perfection. If she didn't know better, she could have sworn she was witnessing a Broadway event.

Okay, maybe she was a bit prejudiced since she produced and directed it. But judging from the number of people who came up to congratulate her, she wasn't the only one who thought the play was a success.

Jordan leaned back against one of the trees at the far end of the park near the back row of chairs, watching the interaction of the cast members with the crowd.

She had to laugh at their antics. One would think Hollywood had descended on Magnolia as one by one the members of the play came out to greet their adoring public. They signed autographs, even if it was for their own friends and neighbors.

Despite her reservations, she'd done it. Had produced and directed her own play. Granted, a small-town venue, but successful nonetheless.

"I'm so proud of you, baby," a husky voice whispered behind her. She turned and smiled as Sam took her in his arms. "You were great."

Wrapping her arms around his waist, she laughed. "They were great. Not me. Wasn't it wonderful?"

"You're wonderful. You've made every single person in this town happy. Are you aware of that? They've wanted this for years, and never could get it off the ground. Until you came here and took over, and brought the people of Magnolia the culture they've been craving."

"Oh please," she said, although she could feel the blush heating her face. "It was just a little play. A bit of entertainment for the Summer Festival. Really no big deal."

Sam shook his head and turned her around to watch the crowd milling about the cast. "You underestimate your talents. It took a lot to put on a production like this. That was a professional job. You should be proud of yourself."

Sighing contentedly, she nodded. "I am proud. Thank you, Sam." She pulled his arms around her and leaned against his chest.

"By the way," he said as he watched the stage with her. "Did you know that Joshua Miller of the *Lincoln Sentinel* was in the audience tonight, taking pictures and making notes for an article he's going to publish in the paper?"

"Really?" The *Lincoln Sentinel*, while certainly not the *New York Times*, was still a large newspaper by many cities' standards. Jordan wondered why the paper would be interested in writing up a review of this small-town play, although she did remember that Joshua was raised in Magnolia.

Looking over her shoulder she eyed Sam suspiciously. "You called him didn't you?"

His eyes widened in disbelief. "Who? Me?"

"Don't act innocent with me. You called Joshua and asked him to come up and review my play didn't you?"

"Maybe. But I didn't tell him how to react, or what to write. No journalist with any integrity will write anything other than their own opinion. You know that as well as I do."

"Well, did he say anything about it? What if he hated it? Oh how could you do this to me?"

Sam laughed at her. "Stop worrying. He told me he loved it. Said it was as professional a production as one could see outside of a major city or Broadway show. He was very impressed with your abilities, and he's going to write that in his review."

Jordan beamed. Okay, maybe it wasn't Broadway. But she couldn't care less. This was a talented group of people, they all worked very hard, and were deserving of all accolades they received. She was proud of what she had done. And enjoyed every minute of it.

"Thank you." She turned and pressed her lips to his in a warm kiss. "I don't want to appear ungrateful, it's just that I hadn't expected this."

"Sometimes life is full of surprises, and we actually end up wanting what we least expected."

That statement certainly had multiple implications.

"Sam, about what you said today—"

"Not now, babe," he said, kissing her forehead. "Your adoring public awaits, and I've monopolized your time long enough. Go, do what you need to do, and we'll have time to talk later."

She couldn't recall ever having had this much fun. After Sam left she wrapped up a few things, talked to some of the audience members who wanted to congratulate her, and was interviewed by Joshua Miller.

Sam was right. Joshua was very impressed with the production, and was sorry to hear that it was only a one-night event. He suggested she put on some encore performances, since his paper was circulated to many of the local towns, both large and small, and there was a dearth of decent plays for the communities to view. He was certain her show would generate a lot of interest and bring people in from the surrounding areas.

She hadn't thought about that before. What would happen if she started a real community theater in this town? What would that mean to her, both professionally and personally? Did she want to stay, or did she want to go back to New York?

Before, there had been nothing to keep her in Magnolia. Now things were different.

Sam told her he loved her. Her heart still soared thinking about it. He loved her. And she loved him, although she had yet to tell him.

As she waited for Sam, Fred and Lois Tanner approached.

"Jordan, it was wonderful," Lois exclaimed. "You must be so pleased."

"I am, Mrs. Tanner. Thank you both so much for coming."

Lois looked surprised. "Why wouldn't we come? We have to support our son's girlfriend, after all."

Girlfriend. Sam's girlfriend. Even his parents saw them as a couple. She couldn't hide the smile on her face.

"What are you planning to do now? Stay in Magnolia, we hope."

Lois voiced what Jordan had been thinking for some time, and yet hearing it made it seem real.

"I don't know yet what I'm going to do. But I'm giving it some thought."

Never one to pass on a matchmaking opportunity, Lois asked, "And are some of your thoughts about our son?"

Hesitating only a moment, she surprised even herself when she answered. "Yes ma'am, they are."

Lois hugged her, and Jordan felt an outpouring of maternal love she'd never felt before. Tears stung her eyes as she thought how nice it would be to have a mother.

"Can I ask you a question?" Lois asked.

"Of course." Jordan sensed it was going to be a serious one.

"How do you honestly feel about Sam?"

Well, that put it right out there didn't it? But it didn't bother her at all to answer.

"I'm in love with him, Mrs. Tanner."

The smile on Lois Tanner's face lit up the night sky. "Oh, honey, I'm so happy to hear that!" She crushed Jordan to her in an even bigger hug, and then reached into her purse for a hankie to dab away the tears. "He needs someone like you in his life. You're the best thing that's happened to him in a very long time."

The tears threatened again, but she kept them at bay. "Thank you, Mrs. Tanner."

Fred placed a hand on her shoulder. "He's a good boy, Jordan. You won't be sorry." Winking at her, he added, "My son's a very lucky man."

After they left, she tried to keep her feet planted on the ground, but it was damned hard when she felt like soaring through the air. Not only did she have a man to love, and who loved her back, but his parents liked her too.

What would happen if she stayed? The idea didn't send her into a panic as it would have a month ago. In fact, remaining in Magnolia seemed more and more appealing each time she thought about it.

She would be giving up her career in New York, though. And her dreams. What about those? Her plans to open her own theater were so close to coming to fruition now. Could she really walk away without giving it a try?

Maybe Sam could come with her to New York.

No, impossible. He'd never do that. Why would he want to live in a big city, when he hated big cities?

Damn. She had a lot more thinking to do about all this. The last thing she wanted to do was let the excitement over the play's success here cloud her logical thinking processes.

One step at a time.

And speaking of that first step, where was Sam? He was supposed to meet her back here about thirty minutes ago and hadn't shown up. She was actually getting excited at the thought of staying in Magnolia and couldn't wait to talk to him about it.

Figured, Mr. Always Prompt would pick now to be late. Rather than continuing to wait, she decided to go find him.

And when she did, the first thing she'd tell him was that she loved him. Then she'd tell him she was thinking about staying, and see how he felt about it. The geography of it all they'd figure out later.

She wandered through the maze of rides and carnival games set up at the end of Main Street. The double Ferris wheel loomed high above the steeple of the First Church of Magnolia, and screams and squeals could be heard emanating from several of the more daring rides interspersed throughout the carnival. Children with sticky cotton candy and caramel apple fingers raced through the walkways adorned with carnival hawkers beckoning players to try their luck to win a prize.

It would be fun to walk through the game booths with Sam. Maybe he'd even win a stuffed animal for her. She giggled at the thought of her and Sam walking hand and hand together, playing games and eating junk food until they were sick. Maybe they'd even ride the Tunnel of Love, a perennial favorite among the teenagers in Magnolia.

And that's how Jordan felt right now. Like a teenager. Only this time, the man of her dreams wasn't just a case of unrequited love. This time he was real.

Reaching the end of the row of rides and booths, she spotted Sam tucked into a corner of one of the buildings. He appeared to be talking to someone, but it was dark and she couldn't see who it was. Although she hated to interrupt him if he was talking business, she walked closer to get his attention and let him know she was there.

The sudden shock of what she saw numbed her immediately. Her heart pounded furiously and tears began to form in her eyes. It couldn't be. Oh God, not this.

Sam was leaning into the doorway, his back to her. Draped all over him was a petite blonde Jordan didn't recognize, her arms wrapped around his neck. Now that she was closer, the streetlight illuminated the couple. The woman was looking up at Sam with a fierce expression of desire.

The present mixed with the past and she was ten years old again, watching her father in the arms of another woman, her mother holding her hand and yanking her along so that she couldn't see.

But she'd seen. And she'd heard their arguments later that night when they thought she was asleep. The same argument she'd heard time and time again. Her mother's sobbing voice begging her father not to see that woman again. Her father laughing, saying he'd do what he damned well pleased.

She couldn't breathe through the intense pain crushing her heart. She tried to suck in air but couldn't manage a complete breath. Her stomach ached and her legs trembled so violently she was afraid she'd fall.

Unable to move, she watched as the woman pressed closer to Sam. She could clearly see her raise up on her toes, her red-painted lips parting as she readied for a kiss.

How could she have been so stupid as to believe Sam could have genuine feelings about her? He was a man, and a man would say and do anything, including lie.

Jordan felt sick, her agony so acute that physical pain pummeled her stomach. Heaving a choked cry and gasping as she sucked in enough air to move, she whipped around and fled.

* * * * *

Sam turned at the sound of Jordan's cry and watched her hurry away. He started to go after her, but his ex-wife held tight to him, refusing to let go.

"Dammit, Penny, I'm not going to tell you again to get your hands off me!" He peeled her hands from around his neck for the third time, finally forcefully pushing her away.

Penny affected a pert pout to her overly painted lips as she held on to Sam's wrist when he would have walked away. "C'mon honey, you know you want me. You always wanted me before. It can be good for us again, you'll see. Just give me another chance."

Glancing desperately at Jordan's retreating form, knowing what she must be thinking, Sam had neither the desire nor the inclination to continue the conversation with his ex-wife. He had, in fact, been trying to extricate himself from her clutches since she'd cornered him ten minutes ago, giving him her sob story about how much she missed him and wanted him back.

The last person he'd ever expected to see in Magnolia was Penny.

"Look," he said impatiently as he jerked his arm away from her. "We're divorced, which is what you wanted. You don't want me, you're just flat broke now and you know I have a successful business which you think you can cash in on."

Not believing the shocked look on Penny's face, he continued. "I feel nothing for you; you wasted your time coming back here. Now I want you to listen to me carefully because I'm not going to say this again. You repulse me. Get the hell out of my life and stay there!"

Without a single backward glance in his ex-wife's direction, despite her crocodile tears and wails, Sam turned and ran off to catch Jordan.

Jordan furiously tried to wipe away the tears that spilled freely as she ran behind the storefronts of Main Street, not wanting anyone to see her crying. She quickened her pace even further when she heard Sam call her name. Try as she might to outrun him, he soon caught up and forced her to stop.

"Jordan, wait!" Sam turned her around to face him. "I know you saw that, and it's not what you think. Let me explain."

Angry with Sam and furious at herself for her stupidity in caring for him, she said, "You don't owe me any explanation. What I saw was perfectly clear." She tried to walk away, but he held her firm.

"That woman you saw me with was my ex-wife, Penny. She came to town today and claimed she wanted me back. I hadn't even seen her until right before you walked up and found her arms around me."

"Great." She couldn't hold back the choked, desperate laugh as she gave up fighting the tears, letting them roll down her face. "I hope you two will be very happy together."

"I don't want her! I want you, Jordan, and I think you know that. I love you."

She hugged her arms to her stomach, trying to control the rising nausea. "So you said. But then you'd say anything to a woman you were sleeping with, wouldn't you? You're no different than my father!"

"That's not true and you know it! I'm nothing like your father, just like you're nothing like your mother."

"Right. Nothing like my father. Except in the morning you tell me you love me, and by evening your hands are all over your ex-wife." She pushed him away as he tried to touch her.

He blew out a forceful sigh. "That's not the way it was at all. She found me and said she had something important to discuss with me. I foolishly agreed to hear her out, and then before I knew it she was all over me, pushing herself against me and telling me how much she missed me. I never had my hands on her, except to peel hers off me."

As much as she wanted to believe him, she couldn't. Men like him were liars and cheats, and would never be satisfied with one woman. She should have known better. Love was a fantasy, that unattainable thing you read about in books but doesn't exist in real life.

She should have known this would happen, would have been better off to keep her distance from Sam. Instead, she'd allowed herself to fall in love with him, and, just like her mother, the man she loved had broken her heart.

Only unlike her mother, she'd never beg. She'd never stay with a man who couldn't keep his zipper closed whenever he was out of her sight. Without trust, they had nothing. And she didn't trust Sam at all.

She needed escape, and she needed it now.

"Jordan! Jordan I'm so glad I found you!" Mavis Riley said breathlessly as she stopped in front of Jordan and Sam. Fortunately it was dark and the woman didn't notice Jordan's red-rimmed eyes or the tears still staining her cheeks. "I've been looking all over for you tonight. We got an offer on your house. Full asking price, and they want to buy it immediately!"

She looked at Sam, who was watching her expectantly. Turning to Mavis, she lifted her chin and nodded. "Accept the offer. Sell the house immediately. It's time for me to get back to New York, anyway."

Mavis thanked her and hurried off. Jordan looked at Sam, a hollow emptiness in her stomach. She felt raw, used, completely exhausted.

Sam looked pained. She wasn't buying it for a second. He was probably thrilled she'd be leaving, figuring he'd accidentally blurted out the whole "I love you" thing and was glad she wasn't going to hold him to it.

"You're leaving," he said flatly.

"Yes, I am."

"Don't go, baby. Not like this. Not when we have so much together."

Eyeing Sam levelly, not wanting to betray the anguish pouring through her body, she said, "Look. It's been fun, but that's all it was. I have a life in New York that I want to get back to."

"That's bullshit and you know it."

If she believed what she saw in his eyes, she'd think he was as hurt as she was right now. But then Sam was obviously a better actor than she was.

"Is it?" She furiously wiped away the tears with the back of her hand, disgusted with herself for letting him know she was hurting.

"Your life is here, with me, in this town. I know it and you know it." He took her hand in his, but Jordan just let it lay loosely in his palm. She felt dead inside, devoid of any feeling. She had to feel that way. Any other way hurt too much.

"I don't know any such thing. You may have had these grandiose ideas about where you and I were headed, but I never did. I knew it would never work out, and I was right. My life isn't here, and it certainly isn't with you.

"This is a small town, Sam, and I hate small towns. Especially this one. You and I had some fun, and that's all. In fact, I was trying to tell you that I didn't love you. I'm sorry, but I don't. You don't have nearly enough to offer me, and my life is in New York. If I stayed here I'd be gone in less than a year."

He dropped her hand as if it was on fire. She could barely meet his gaze, seeing the hurt in his eyes that she knew was a lie. He didn't hurt. To hurt he'd have to care, and he didn't care for her at all. Not like she thought he did. She was just another roll in the hay to him, another playmate until a better one came along.

He glared at her through those eyes of false pain, anger replacing the hurt. "I'm sorry you don't trust me enough to know that my feelings for you are real. Sorry you're going to throw away what we could have together. But I can't make you trust in me or my love for you,

Jordan. That you'll have to figure out on your own." He walked away, leaving her standing in the alley alone.

Just the way she'd always been. Alone. She liked it that way, right?

Leaning against the wall, she crouched down, laid her face in her hands, and let the racking sobs overtake her.

* * * * *

Sam threw his keys on his desk as he entered the office, preferring the darkness to turning on any lights.

Jordan didn't have faith in him, didn't trust him. Sure, he could understand it looked bad, it would have looked bad to anyone who would have walked in on that scene and found Penny draped all over him. But he'd told her how he felt, told her he loved her. And to Jordan, it had meant nothing.

Just like Penny.

Damn his ex-wife. He poured a glass of bourbon and sat down behind his desk, propping his feet on the top and leaning back in his chair. Her sense of lousy timing had always been impeccable.

Typical of Penny to go where the money was. She was even willing to try living in Magnolia again, she said, just because she realized how much she loved him. The thought made him laugh. Right. And he just fell off the turnip truck yesterday.

She'd always thought him stupid. That was her biggest mistake, and obviously she hadn't learned a damn thing since they split up. She sure as hell hadn't learned about love.

Penny had never loved anything in her life except money and excitement. And the guy she left him for had provided both, including an expensive lifestyle in Dallas, the big city she craved. That is until her new lover's business went bankrupt, and Penny was forced to sacrifice. A word definitely not in her vocabulary.

So she thought she'd try her luck with her ex again. Well not this time. He may have been stupid once but he was smarter than most. Just having her hands on him tonight made his skin crawl.

How could he have ever thought she was attractive? She wore way too much makeup and dressed like a tramp. And he never noticed before how cold her eyes were.

Every moment he looked at Penny he was reminded of the warmth and light in Jordan's emerald eyes, her soft skin, the way he felt when she touched him, the pleasure he received when he touched her. Jordan gave as much as Sam did, didn't hold back her feelings.

Sam had wanted only to get away from Penny and find the woman he loved. But the woman he loved saw Penny throwing herself at him, and assumed he was reciprocating.

Regardless of how it looked, anyone who cared for him, who really knew him, would know it wasn't in his nature to cheat or lie.

Fuck!

Maybe he'd been wrong about Jordan. Maybe she wasn't the right woman for him all along. She didn't trust him, in fact never had. And probably never would. He was better off without her.

So why did he ache so damn much right now? Why did his heart feel like a fist was wrapped around it, squeezing the life, the love, out of it?

Because despite how she felt about him, he loved her. Loved her like he had never loved another woman. And now she was leaving him, leaving Magnolia, and leaving a hole in his heart that would never heal.

Downing the contents of his glass in one gulp, he welcomed the burning in his chest, hoping it would mask the ache in his heart.

Chapter Thirteen

The doorbell rang just as Jordan finished organizing her things to pack. She ran downstairs, not really knowing who would be there but foolishly hoping it was the one person she didn't really want to see.

She tried to mask her disappointment as she pulled the door open to find Katie. Putting on her best smile, she invited her in.

"You're really leaving?" Katie motioned to the suitcases sitting at the bottom of the stairs as they walked down the hall towards the kitchen.

"Yes, it's time for me to go. The house is sold and the new owners want a short closing period, so I have to be out today."

"I can't believe you're really going to leave. I thought you were happy here, Jordan. I thought maybe with the success of the play you'd want to stay. And most importantly," Katie said as she took the chair Jordan offered in the kitchen, "I thought you and Sam had something special together, and if nothing else, he'd be the reason you stayed."

Jordan busied herself pouring tea, avoiding eye contact with Katie. "Sam and I have nothing together. We had some fun, and that was all."

"What is it? I can tell you're upset."

"Nothing, really. Just a little stressed trying to get everything done before I leave."

The look on Katie's face showed her disbelief. "That's not it. Talk to me."

"There's really nothing to—"

"Jordan," Katie interrupted. "Tell me."

Sighing, she sat at the table, no longer able to hide the pain she was feeling. "I found Sam with his ex-wife at the Summer Festival."

"I heard Penny came back. Found them doing what?"

"Penny had her arms all over Sam, and his were on her," she said and quickly relayed what she saw that night, trying not to relive the pain that stabbed her moment she found the man she loved in the arms of his ex-wife. "Sam said it was nothing, that it was all her doing and he didn't want any part of it."

"You didn't believe him, did you?"

"No."

Katie took a deep breath. "I can't believe Sam would do anything to deliberately hurt you. He cares deeply for you, all of us can see that. And it's not in his nature to be a two-timer. Especially not with Penny. He learned his lesson a long time ago with her. I know for a fact he doesn't want any part of her."

"I know what I saw," Jordan said defiantly.

"I'm sure you think you saw something, and I wouldn't put it past Penny to put the moves on Sam again. I also know Sam." With an admonishing look, she added. "And you should, too."

She let her anger surface. It was so much easier to be angry than hurt. "What should I know? That he's like my father? That I never should have trusted him in the first

213

place? Never should have..." She couldn't finish the sentence, but Katie finished it for her.

"Never should have fallen in love with him, you mean? Are you in love with Sam?"

The tears fell despite her attempt to keep them at bay. She nodded, unable to speak and feeling stupid for her weakness.

Katie leaned over and put her arms around her. Finally Jordan let go of the emotions she'd held in check for the past few days, crying bucketfuls of tears and misery until she could barely breathe. Katie held her until the storm passed, then got up to grab some tissues and a cold cloth.

"If you love him, then you have to trust him."

With a negative shake of her head, Jordan said, "Love is a fantasy. A woman will believe a man loves her only to find out later that he lied. They're only faithful until someone else catches their eye. Then they're off to the next woman. Just like my father."

"Sam's nothing like your father."

"He's exactly like my father."

Katie heaved a sigh. "Jordan, if you're ever going to find love—real love, you'll have to learn to trust. And you can trust Sam. I know it."

"I appreciate that, Katie, I really do. But I just...can't. Not now. Maybe not ever." The realization hit her like a cold slap in the face. She'd never be able to trust a man.

"You have to let go of the past sometime. Let your parents go. Theirs was a mistake from the beginning, but it has nothing to do with you. You can't judge all men by your father."

When she turned her head away, Katie grabbed her shoulders, forcing her to look her in the eye. "You have a chance to have the kind of love most people only dream of. As your friend I'm going to tell you this one last time. Don't be stupid. Don't walk away from someone who loves you. You'll end up alone and miserable."

* * * * *

Alone and miserable. One week back in New York, and that's exactly how Jordan felt. Thinking distance would be the best thing for her, she couldn't wait to return to the familiar sights and sounds of New York City. Get back to work, get busy, and get her mind off Sam.

And her dream, the one she dreamt for so long, was finally in reach. She'd made enough money on the sale of the house to invest in her own theater. But she couldn't muster up enough enthusiasm to care. In fact, the whole idea of starting a theater in New York no longer held any appeal.

Every time she thought about the money, her mind strayed to what she could build in Magnolia. The type of community theater that would bring revenues into a small town. With the diverse talents available there, let alone who she might find from the surrounding communities, she might have created a wonderful little theater right in her hometown. But that wasn't her dream.

And wasn't she supposed to stick to her goals? Pining after the man she'd lost would be something her mother would have done.

She wasn't her mother.

So she'd loved, and she'd lost. Big deal. She'd get over it. For years she'd done just fine without a man in her life.

It was time to get back to work, and forget about romance, about sex, about everything and anything having to do with Sam Tanner.

Right now she was busy trying to catch up, getting used to a new director. Clive Latrelle. The man was a tyrant, bellowing out orders and never satisfied with anything. Jordan could barely stand to work with him. Clive would be directing the new play for the next few months and would probably get worse. Directors like him always did. But it was her job.

She hated it. Hated her job, hated New York, hated the fact that not a single soul knew anything about her. She could die and no one would notice she was missing. She had no real friends. No one waved or said hello to her as she walked down the street. No friendly faces welcomed her when she walked into a store. No one here even knew her. She had no close girlfriends like Katie, no one she could confide in or just hang out with. Jordan was a stranger among a million people, instead of a friend and neighbor to hundreds.

But it was more than that.

She missed Sam so much she thought she'd die. Distance didn't help erase the pain of being away from him. It only served to remind her how much she loved him, how much she needed him.

Lonely nights in her apartment gave her time to think about Sam, about what happened between the two of them. Had Katie been right? Was she completely wrong about what she'd seen that night in the alley?

In order to believe that Sam had been telling the truth, she'd have to trust.

Trust didn't come easy, especially relating to men. Too many years watching men play her mother for a fool had taught her not to put her faith in anything a man said.

Her mother had always had hope. Hope that the new guy she dallied with would be the right one, and when that didn't work out, hope that the next one would be better.

She'd hoped her way right into an early grave, miserably unhappy.

No way would Jordan trust implicitly.

Then again, she wasn't her mother. Her mother just wanted too much; her dreams were too big. She searched for a perfect man, and one didn't exist. When she didn't find him, she found fault with the ones she was with, eventually driving them all away.

Did Jordan do the same thing to Sam? Had she been so convinced that she was right and he was wrong that she purposely walked away from something that could have been wonderful?

Why would he tell her he loved her and then take up with another woman the same day?

That didn't make sense.

That kind of behavior *wasn't* Sam.

Oh, God. He had told her the truth. His ex-wife had thrown herself at him in an attempt to reconcile.

None of this had been Sam's fault. It had been hers. Her own fears, her own inability to trust. He'd given her his heart and she'd stomped all over it and threw it back at him, then made it worse by calling him a liar.

She hadn't believed that he loved her.

How could Sam love her? Her own mother hadn't loved her enough to stay with her.

God, she needed a shrink. How stupid was she? She had the man of her dreams in the palm of her hand and she blew him away like dust.

And now she was back in New York, with way too much time on her hands to think. Think about what was happening in Magnolia. Missing the familiar sights and smells of Belle Coeur. Missing the man who had shared her bed, who had shared her life.

New York was no longer her haven, her hiding place from real feelings and emotion. If nothing else, it only reminded her how empty her life had been before she returned to Magnolia. She'd buried herself so deeply in her career that she'd forgotten what was really important.

Now she knew what she was missing. Friendship, neighbors, people who knew and cared about her, and most importantly, love.

All these years she'd wondered what it was like to have a real, traditional family. Oh sure, she'd had Grandma, and Grandma had given her all the love and family one person could. Had she opened her eyes and her heart she would have realized that the entire town of Magnolia was her family.

All the years wondering what it was like to love someone. Someone who loved her back. She'd had that. With Sam.

Katie was right. The kind of love most people never experienced had been hers for the taking, and she'd foolishly let it go. But was it too late? Could she still have a chance at happiness, the kind her mother searched for and never found? Did she have the guts enough to try?

She was tired of thinking about it. Tired of being inactive, too paralyzed by fear to reach out for what she really wanted. No more. It was time for her to grow up, take a chance, even if she failed. She'd at least know she tried.

It was time for Jordan to put her parents' pain to rest, and live her own life.

"Miss Weston!" Clive Latrelle bellowed down at her as she sat in the first row of seats making notes. "Where is my tea? I expressly instructed my tea was to be brought to me at precisely ten a.m. It is now ten minutes after ten and I do not see it. Bring it to me now!"

Assistant Director, her behind. Jordan wasn't an assistant, she was his personal maid.

"Miss Weston, are you deaf? Now, woman, now!"

That was it. She calmly placed her clipboard in the seat beside her, walked up the stairs to the stage and approached him. Clive was a short, pudgy-faced little gnome with a receding hairline and a huge ego. She'd bet he had a dick the size of pencil eraser, too. Smiling sweetly at him, she replied, "Get it yourself."

Clive's face reddened in surprise and anger. "What?"

Jordan sensed a hissy fit of epic proportions was about to take place.

"You heard me," she replied calmly. "Get it yourself, you pompous, egotistical, bald-headed old fool. I quit." She turned and walked from the theater, smiling as she heard Clive sputtering curses at her retreating form.

"Miss Weston! Where are you going?"

Jordan threw her head back and laughed with pure joy. "Home," she said to herself as she walked out the door. "I'm going home."

* * * * *

Another day, Sam thought as he pulled his truck into the parking spot in front of TNT. Another mundane day. Go to work, work until you're so exhausted you can't think, then collapse at home and try to sleep. Trouble was, sleep wasn't coming. Hadn't come since Jordan left.

God, he missed her. More than he thought he would. When she left, he was crushed. Pissed off. Disappointed that she didn't have enough faith in him to trust him. But still he missed her. He even foolishly looked for her on the street every day, hoping to see her red hair flying as she turned the corner.

Foolish was right. She was gone. Back to New York, her big city. Back to where she was happy. As far away from Sam as she could get.

Snap out of it man! Get a grip and get on with your life. She isn't coming back. Your love wasn't enough for her, so let her go.

Cookie forced a tremulous smile as he entered the office. He barely grumbled a hello as he walked past, went into his office and closed the door.

Sam felt bad because he knew he'd been grumpy lately. He barked at Cookie, yelled at his crew, and Tony was so pissed at him he threatened to deck him next time Sam said a surly word. Oh yeah, he was pure joy to be around these days. No wonder no one bothered to knock at his door after he arrived in the mornings. They really didn't want to be around him. He didn't blame them—he could barely stand himself.

All because Jordan had gone back to New York. And he wanted her back.

But he hadn't done a goddamned thing about getting her back.

An idea formed in his sleep-deprived mind. A really stupid idea, but one that refused to go away.

If he flew to New York to see her, stayed there for a few days and tried to convince her of his love, maybe she'd come back.

But what if she didn't? Jordan loved New York, loved living in a large city. Was it fair of him to love a woman with all his heart, yet expect her to make all the sacrifices? Why couldn't he make the sacrifice?

Of course it would mean moving. To a large city. Something he swore he'd never do.

He remembered thinking to himself not long ago that love wasn't fair. He loved Jordan, and wanted her back. If he had to move to New damn York then that's what he'd do. He certainly had plenty of money to start his own business there, if he liquidated his assets in Magnolia.

A loud knock at the door to his office was followed by Tony throwing it open so hard it hit the wall with a loud crack. Sam jumped up, prepared for battle.

"What the hell do you think you're doing? Get out and leave me alone!"

Completely ignoring his outburst, Tony flopped down in the chair in front of Sam's desk and leaned back comfortably, grinning from ear to ear.

"What are you grinning about? You get laid last night and want to share the good news? Thanks but no thanks. I don't want to hear about it."

Tony threw his head back and laughed. "I get laid almost every night, partner. And I never kiss and tell."

Sam couldn't help but smile at Tony's cockiness. A true friend as well as a partner, it didn't matter one whit to Tony whether Sam was in a bad mood or not. If Tony was in a good one, which he usually was, he always shared it.

"Sit down and relax. I'm not here to fight with you. At least not today. Keep pissing me off though, and I might take you on tomorrow."

Sam shot Tony a hard look, barely keeping the corners of his mouth from forming a grin. "I'd kick your ass."

"Dream on, old man."

"Give me a break. I'm six months older than you are."

"Exactly. Too old to take me on."

Banter like this was exactly what he needed to snap him out of his misery. It didn't make it go away, but at least helped push thoughts of Jordan aside momentarily.

"What's on the agenda today?"

Tony shrugged. "Same stuff as yesterday. Oh, except for one thing."

"What?" Hopefully it was new business. Starting a new project would certainly help take his mind off feeling sorry for himself.

"Katie asked if you could come by the theater and look at the stage. Seems it might need some refurbishing or something."

Great. Another reminder of Jordan—just what he didn't need right now. "Can't you take care of it?"

Tony shook his head. "Nope. That one's all yours. I have to supervise a crew down at London's Millhouse. They're getting ready to put up the skeleton, so I need to be there. Anyway, I already told Katie you'd pop over this morning to take a look."

Katie had temporarily taken over director's duties at the theater after Jordan left, until another could be found. Although no one was anxious to find a replacement for Jordan.

Sighing, he nodded. "Fine. I'll go take a look now, before I get wrapped up in something else." Seeing Tony's grin, Sam looked at him quizzically. "What are you so happy about this morning?"

"It's just a great day and I'm happy," Tony said with an annoying grin.

"Well spread it somewhere else," Sam growled. "You're beginning to piss me off."

Tony winked at him. "That's the idea."

"While you're here, I have a question for you."

"Okay. Shoot."

"If I were to sell my half of TNT Construction, would you be willing to buy me out?"

Tony arched a brow. "You thinking of selling?"

"Maybe."

"Why?"

"I might be considering a move."

Leaning back in the chair, Tony crossed his arms over his chest. "Really? Where?"

"New York."

"I see." Tony was silent for a few minutes, his expression unreadable. Then his lips tilted in a sly smile. "We can talk about it."

Sam nodded. "Okay. I'm going to be gone a few days, too. I have some personal business to take care of, so we'll discuss this when I get back."

"Sure, partner. Whatever you want. Just let me know when you're ready."

Tony stood and walked out of the office, singing one of the songs from *The Music Man*. Sam didn't quite understand why his partner was smiling so smugly at him, but didn't really have time to think about it.

While heading down the block toward the theater, he started to make plans. After he met with Katie, he'd make arrangements to fly to New York tomorrow, and camp out on Jordan's doorstep until she let him in. Then he'd tell her he loved her, over and over again until she believed him.

Once they got past that, he'd tell her he was moving to New York to be with her.

He opened the door to the theater. It was dark inside. No answer when he called out Katie's name either. Well, hell. The last thing he needed was a delay. There were things he needed to take care of. He headed through the doors to the small auditorium, finding a single light shining on the makeshift stage.

Katie ran out into the spotlight, sporting the same idiotic grin Tony had.

"Take a seat, Sam," Katie shouted. "I'll be right with you." Then she disappeared backstage. He could have sworn she was giggling.

He sat down and looked around. He felt Jordan everywhere. Every time he looked at this place he was reminded of her. God, he could even smell her perfume. His head dropped to his chest and he heaved a huge sigh.

"Sam."

His head whipped up at the sound of Jordan's voice. He couldn't believe it was really her, standing center stage in the spotlight. But it was. Dressed in a blue cotton sundress and sandals, her hair falling loosely around her shoulders, she was like a dream. Real or not, she was a vision that took his breath away.

But what was she doing back here?

Jordan took a deep breath. She'd rehearsed over and over what she was going to say to Sam, but now that he was here she couldn't remember any of it.

Sam walked up the steps to the stage, stopping a few feet away from her.

"What are you doing here?"

"I came back," she replied nervously.

"Why?"

"I missed you."

"I see." He moved closer until he was only inches away. She drank in the sight and crisp, male scent of him, feeling like it had been years instead of weeks since she'd seen him. Now, as she looked at his tanned face, gorgeous turquoise eyes and full sensuous lips, she wanted nothing more than to wrap herself around him and never let go.

"I want you, Sam," she admitted. "I...I was wrong not to trust you. My parents' relationship has gotten in my way my whole life. I thought if I fell in love with someone, I'd end up like my mother."

"And did you?"

"Did I what?"

"Did you fall in love?"

She took the single step necessary to walk into his arms and change her life.

"Yes, Sam. I fell in love. With you."

She slid her arms around his neck and pressed her mouth against his, asking him without words to take her back. He pulled her close and plundered her mouth, searing her with the touch of their lips. She kissed him with all the pent-up longing of the past few weeks, telling him in that kiss what was in her heart. All the love, and all the trust she could give him.

Sam finally broke the kiss, and slid his thumb over the tear that escaped her eye.

"Jordan, I'm moving to New York."

What was he talking about? "What?"

"You heard me. I love you, and I want to be with you. But it wouldn't be fair to ask you to sacrifice your dream for me. I know how you feel about New York, how much you love it there. Once I sell my half of TNT to Tony, I'll have plenty of capital to start a business in New York. Hell, they're always building something there."

She was too shocked to speak. The man who hated big cities, who'd ended a marriage because he refused to move to one, was offering to completely change his life for her. Her heart pounded in her chest as the realization hit her.

He really did love her.

"I hate New York," she replied, a smile curving her lips.

Sam's eyes widened. "You do?"

"Yes. I just didn't realize it until I got back there. Magnolia is my home, Sam. I'm here because this is where I want to be. With you. This is my dream."

He pulled her into his arms, kissing her senseless.

"I love you," she said, the tears now falling in earnest.

"I love you too, baby. God, I missed you so much when you left."

They held each other for a moment, then Sam gently backed away. "I want to ask you a question."

"Okay." She wondered why he was doing getting down on the floor, then she realized what was happening. Chills broke out all over her body as Sam got on one knee, taking her hand in his.

She couldn't believe this was happening. Her legs were shaking and her heart beat so fast she was afraid she'd hyperventilate.

"Jordan Lee Weston, I love you with all my heart. Will you marry me?"

For the first time in her life, completely without hesitation, she felt truly loved.

"Yes," she said through the tears. "I love you too, Sam Ethan Tanner, with all my heart. I would be honored to marry you."

A round of applause broke out. She turned to see all their friends at the back of the theater, shouting congratulations and applauding Sam's proposal. The entire cast of the play was there, along with Millie, Katie and Tony, who stood in the front row of the crowd, arms crossed, huge satisfied smiles on their faces.

She grinned at her friends, those matchmaking busybodies who wouldn't leave them alone. She had them to thank for pounding the truth into her head.

Instead of rushing the stage to congratulate them, they slipped out the door, leaving Jordan and Sam alone.

"I feel the need to celebrate with you," Sam said with a gleam in his eye.

Jordan raised an eyebrow. "Celebrate, huh? That can only mean one thing."

He laughed and picked her up, showering her with kisses. "Let's go home." The sensuous tone in his voice signaled his readiness to consummate their engagement.

"We'll have to go to your place," she replied. "As of yet, I don't have a home."

Sam grinned like a little boy who just hit his first home run. "Yeah, you do."

"No, I don't. Remember? I sold Belle Coeur." Her smile faded. "That's what I regret the most. I foolishly sold Grandma's house. I thought I wanted money to start my own theater, and I sold the home I loved to get it. Now I've lost it."

Sam kissed the tip of her nose. "No, you haven't."

She didn't understand. "What do you mean?"

"I bought the house. I've always loved that old place, and when I realized I loved you I wanted to make it our home."

He'd bought Belle Coeur. For her. For the two of them. No wonder she loved him so much. "Oh Sam, I can't believe you did that." The waterworks started again, but she didn't care.

Sam wiped the tears from her face, and kissed her. "A man in love knows exactly what his woman needs, even if said stubborn, mule-headed woman doesn't always listen to reason."

She laughed, her heart soaring free with the fullness of her love for him. "I can't wait to marry you, Sam. I want to have children with you and share our lives here in Magnolia. One built on trust and the love we feel for each other."

Sam wrapped his arms around her. "Let's go home. To Belle Coeur."

She could barely sit still as they made the drive up the long path leading to the house.

Home. For the first time, no ghosts of the past greeted her, only the love that her grandmother had always showed her in the past, and the love she felt for the man clutching her hand and leading her up the stairs.

"I'd like to do this right, but I can't wait any longer," he said as soon as they opened the door.

She knew what he wanted, because she wanted it too.

"Hurry up then," she teased. "I haven't had sex in…weeks."

He laughed, swooping her off her feet and into his arms and heading into the great room. "I've always wanted to fuck you here, over that antique couch. Are you scandalized?"

With an arched brow, she fanned her face with her hand and dredged up her handy southern belle accent. "Why, Mr. Tanner, surely you don't mean to ravage me right here in the parlor."

"Yes, ma'am, I do."

Then no words were necessary as the look on Sam's face was more than enough to fire her libido to a fever-pitch. He jerked the dress up and flipped her around, bending her over the back of the couch. Her panties were quickly disposed of, his jeans were dropped to the floor and a hot, hard male body pressed against her buttocks.

He reached between her legs and caressed her slit, probing, relentlessly stroking and caressing her until her juices spilled onto his fingers. He situated himself between her legs and thrust inside her.

She came immediately, all the pent-up anxiety and emotion flying away in the face of exhilarating pleasure. But he didn't stop, instead continued to pound at her sex, hard and fast, until his balls slapped against her clit and took her over the edge again. When his climax hit him, he grabbed her hips and ground against her, spilling inside her again and again until his come poured down her quivering legs.

Spent, she could only lie there draped over the couch until Sam pulled her upright, massaging her lower back and kissing the nape of her neck.

She shivered, turned and wrapped her arms around his neck.

"This old house is never going to be the same again," she teased.

"It has a lot of rooms. I intend to fuck you in each one of them, more than once."

Somehow she already knew their lives together would never be dull. She wouldn't have it any other way.

Epilogue
Two Years Later

Jordan couldn't contain her cheesy grin as she held the oversized scissors in her hands.

"Need some help with that?"

She looked up lovingly at her husband. Sam smiled, his eyes filled with love and pride. Every time Jordan looked at him her heart soared.

"Since you built it, I think it's appropriate that you help me cut the ribbon."

He placed his much larger hands over hers, and together they sliced through the big satin ribbon signaling the grand opening of the Magnolia Performing Arts Center.

The applause rang out as almost everyone in town cheered and clapped loudly.

She took a deep breath and fought back tears as she looked at the imposing structure in front of her. The large brick building was just another one of the many dreams that had come true for Jordan in the past couple years.

TNT Construction had done a wonderful job. The theater was huge, with a graduated audience section fifty rows in depth. It even had an orchestra pit. And the stage — now that was comparable to any New York theater. Trap doors, lights, sound, everything she could have ever wanted was there.

And it was hers. Her theater. Not just a storefront with a makeshift stage in the back room. But an honest to God performing arts center.

She wiped her cheeks with the back of her hand and felt a tug at her long skirt.

"Damma."

She looked down at Violet, her one-year-old daughter, and smiled as Sam snuck up behind the child and swept her into his arms.

"Damma!" she said excitedly, waving her chubby hands in the air as she squealed with delight.

"Think she'll ever say momma or dada separately, or will it always be a combo?"

Sam laughed. "Don't know. Don't care. She's perfect either way. Besides, we *are* a combo."

She had to agree. Watching father and daughter, so similar in looks with their dark hair and turquoise eyes, made the tears well again.

How lucky she was. She had everything she ever wanted. Everything she'd dreamed about was hers.

Her theater. Friends and family to love. A husband she loved more than her own life, a child of their love at her side.

Sam put Violet on his shoulders and grabbed Jordan's hand as they followed the crowd into the theater for punch and cake.

"Sam, do you think fate had anything to do with us getting together?" Jordan remembered George Lewiston saying fate had brought her to Magnolia, but didn't believe it then. Now she did. She believed she was fated to return to Magnolia, fall in love with Sam, and build her theater right here in her hometown.

"I don't know about fate, baby, but I know about dreams."

His eyes held hers, his gaze still filled with the same passion for her as it had over two years ago. The same passion she felt for him. Never diminishing, always growing.

"I dreamt of a woman like you my whole life. I dreamt about *you* my whole life. Wanted you, needed you, even when I didn't know it. And my dreams came true."

Pressing a kiss to her lips, he leaned his head against hers. "And I'll spend the rest of my life making yours come true."

She smiled up at the man she loved so much. "You already have, Sam."

"I love you."

"I love you too, Sam. Thank you for making my dreams come true."

As they walked hand in hand into the new building, Jordan realized fate had indeed played a part in her life. Her dream had always been her theater, the only one she allowed herself to have. In her wildest dreams she never thought she'd find love with the man of her heart.

But fate had altered her dreams, and had given her the gift of love.

Enjoy this excerpt from
TANGLED WEB
© Copyright Jaci and CJ Burton 2004

Elexis sighed. What a day. Hell, what a month, for that matter. When the entire security of Earth depended upon a computer system, something going wrong was a big damn deal not only to all humans, but also to the aliens who now governed their planet. And there was no bigger deal than a breach to the system.

To say she was keyed up was an understatement. The entire GIS tech unit had worked diligently the past few months trying to keep the Underground hackers out of the system. Elexis was exhausted from the amount of time she'd spent constantly upgrading the system.

The Underground had made steady gains over the years and had successfully breached the tightest security program on the planet several times. Somebody on the other side was very, very smart.

But not as smart as GIS. She and her coworkers would outwit the hackers and keep the system safe. They always had.

She rolled her neck from side to side to ease the tension and played a few games on the web, neither of which served to alleviate the stress making her chest feel like a tight band wound around it. She needed to relax or she'd never sleep, and tomorrow was another busy day.

What she really needed was an orgasm, a sure tension reliever. It'd been days since she'd sought out cybersex. Tonight would be a perfect night for it. Situating herself onto the wide chaise in front of her system, she spoke her code and waited for the net to come online.

Adjusting the robe so that it covered her legs, she leaned back and reached for her glass of Relaid. She sipped the clear red liquor, enjoying the sweet taste as it burned its way down her throat. Maybe it wasn't real alcohol — the aliens had outlawed that long ago, but it still provided enough chemical relaxation that she could feel the tension in her shoulders slowly easing. Now she was ready to give the next command to the computer.

"Cybersex, please."

The computer answered. "What is your preference?"

Elexis leaned back and closed her eyes, trying to decide. She'd occasionally chosen females to cybersex with, as they understood a woman's body and the triggers to orgasm, but she definitely preferred men. Something about their voices. So deep, so seductive, the husky tones made her libido flame to life.

"Male, between twenty-five and thirty-five. Over six-feet tall. Well built, but not overly muscled. Dark hair, deep voice." She didn't know why she had this vision of a certain man, but it was one she called upon again and again. Not that it made any difference what they looked like. She'd never see them anyway. A series of conversations resulting in a quick orgasm and she'd be satisfied and on her way to bed.

"One moment," the computer answered.

She often wondered what her partners really looked like. Chosen at random, they could be anyone on the planet. All humans lived in alien-controlled high rises occupied by thousands in each building. It could even be a neighbor for all she knew.

Since sex was controlled by the government and identities were kept secret, there'd be no chance of physical contact and recognition later. She never knew who she'd get on the other end of the connection. It could even be someone she worked with.

Thank the government for anonymity. She'd die of embarrassment if she could actually see the person with whom she had sex.

She selected soft jazz music, the slow, sexy strains of a saxophone always putting her in the mood. She'd always enjoyed the old twentieth-century jazz sounds, finding them both sensually stimulating and relaxing at the same time.

An image came up, a rainbow of distorted waves undulating across the screen before it slowly took shape. As always, the figure was more shadow than form, but she could vaguely see a man seated in front of his computer.

"Hello?" she asked.

He didn't answer right away. Finally, he said, "Well, hello there."

His voice warmed her more than the liquor. Deep, husky, dripping with barely leashed sexuality, just the way she liked it. "I'm Lexi. Are you agreeable to cybersex this evening?"

Once again he paused before answering. She leaned forward, wondering if she'd been misdirected and would need to sever their connection. With the upgrades they'd been working on the past few months, anything was possible, even a glitch in the system. Although that was highly unlikely. She was too good at her job to make a mistake like that.

"Cybersex, huh? Sure."

Ah, much better. "What's your name?"

"Cade."

Elexis settled back against the chaise, anticipation knotting her stomach. She opened a drawer filled with toys, trying to decide if she wanted to use her hand or one of the many vibrators guaranteed to send her quickly over the edge.

"Hello Cade. Shall we get started?"

About the author:

Jaci Burton has been a dreamer and lover of romance her entire life. Consumed with stories of passion, love and happily ever afters, she finally pulled her fantasy characters out of her head and put them on paper. Writing allows her to showcase the rainbow of emotions that result from falling in love.

Jaci lives in Oklahoma with her husband (her fiercest writing critic and sexy inspiration), stepdaughter and three wild and crazy dogs. Her sons are grown and live on opposite coasts and don't bother her nearly as often as she'd like them to. When she isn't writing stories of passion and romance, she can usually be found at the gym, reading a great book, or working on her computer, trying to figure out how she can pull more than twenty-four hours out of a single day.

Jaci welcomes mail from readers. You can write to her c/o Ellora's Cave Publishing at 1337 Commerce Drive, Suite 13, Stow OH 44224.

Why an electronic book?

We live in the Information Age—an exciting time in the history of human civilization in which technology rules supreme and continues to progress in leaps and bounds every minute of every hour of every day. For a multitude of reasons, more and more avid literary fans are opting to purchase e-books instead of paperbacks. The question to those not yet initiated to the world of electronic reading is simply: *why?*

1. *Price.* An electronic title at Ellora's Cave Publishing runs anywhere from 40-75% less than the cover price of the <u>exact same title</u> in paperback format. Why? Cold mathematics. It is less expensive to publish an e-book than it is to publish a paperback, so the savings are passed along to the consumer.

2. *Space.* Running out of room to house your paperback books? That is one worry you will never have with electronic novels. For a low one-time cost, you can purchase a handheld computer designed specifically for e-reading purposes. Many e-readers are larger than the average handheld, giving you plenty of screen room. Better yet, hundreds of titles can be stored within your new library—a single microchip. (Please note that Ellora's Cave does not endorse any specific brands. You can check our website at www.ellorascave.com for customer recommendations we make available to new consumers.)

3. *Mobility.* Because your new library now consists of only a microchip, your entire cache of books can be taken with you wherever you go.

4. *Personal preferences are accounted for.* Are the words you are currently reading too small? Too large? Too...**ANNOYING**? Paperback books cannot be modified according to personal preferences, but e-books can.

5. *Innovation.* The way you read a book is not the only advancement the Information Age has gifted the literary community with. There is also the factor of what you can read. Ellora's Cave Publishing will be introducing a new line of interactive titles that are available in e-book format only.

6. *Instant gratification.* Is it the middle of the night and all the bookstores are closed? Are you tired of waiting days—sometimes weeks—for online and offline bookstores to ship the novels you bought? Ellora's Cave Publishing sells instantaneous downloads 24 hours a day, 7 days a week, 365 days a year. Our e-book delivery system is 100% automated, meaning your order is filled as soon as you pay for it.

Those are a few of the top reasons why electronic novels are displacing paperbacks for many an avid reader. As always, Ellora's Cave Publishing welcomes your questions and comments. We invite you to email us at service@ellorascave.com or write to us directly at: 1337 Commerce Drive, Suite 13, Stow OH 44224.

Discover for yourself why readers can't get enough of the multiple award-winning publisher Ellora's Cave. Whether you prefer e-books or paperbacks, be sure to visit EC on the web at www.ellorascave.com for an erotic reading experience that will leave you breathless.

WWW.ELLORASCAVE.COM